BEDLAM

ALLY KENNEN

mlb
MARION LLOYD BOOKS

For Maeve, my number one

Marion Lloyd Books
An imprint of Scholastic Children's Books
Euston House, 24 Eversholt Street
London, NW1 1DB, UK
A division of Scholastic Ltd.
Registered office: Westfield Road, Southam, Warwickshire, CV47 0RA
SCHOLASTIC and associated logos are trademarks and/or registered
trademarks of Scholastic Inc.

First published in the UK in 2009 by Marion Lloyd Books.
This edition published in the UK in 2010 by Marion Lloyd Books.

ISBN 9781407117102

Printed by CPI Bookmarque Ltd, Croydon, Surrey
Papers used by Scholastic Children's Books
are made from wood grown in sustainable forests.

1 3 5 7 9 10 8 6 4 2

www.scholastic.co.uk/zone

CONTENTS

Mother and Dad

Mother says girls shouldn't go out at night. She has a lot of opinions about a lot of things. And when I arrive in her deadly village having not seen her for ages, I'm determined to make a Good Start. But the first thing Mother says when I walk through the door with my suitcases is, "You've put on so much weight, Lexi."

I pause. This is not what I, Lexi Juby, need to hear. Good Start, Good Start, Good Start.

"It looks like it's in the genes," I reply, though Mother, as ever, is slim and immaculate. Her dog is barking wildly in the kitchen. It sounds as mad as if it'd been shut in there with a roomful of cats. Over the din I hear tyres squealing off up the road and turn to watch Dad burn off. All the times I've visited Mother over the years, Dad's never made it past the front gate.

"Hello, Lexi," says Owen, Mother's boyfriend, watching me from the hallway. He gives me the creeps; he always has. I shouldn't have worn this outfit. I should have put on something four sizes too big. He stoops to kiss me but I pretend I have something stuck in my throat and the moment passes.

1

"You've grown up,'" he says, sucking a sweet. "Not a little girl any more. You should be a model."

"Gee, thanks, I'd love to spend my life chucking up my lunch," I say. He prises my suitcases from my fingers. "What a gentleman," I mutter. Owen's a big chap and quite good-looking. I'd find him much easier to deal with if he was ugly. Mother leads us upstairs. I walk up sideways with my bag bumping against my hip to make it difficult for Owen to see up my skirt. I get a surprise, as Mother's had my room redone. Everything is white; the bedspread, the walls, even the carpet. There's a massive black and white print of Manhattan covering one wall and a full-length mirror by the bed. Mother doesn't know this, but I've always wanted to go to New York.

Owen dumps the suitcases on the carpet. "I'll leave you girls to bond," he says.

There's an awkward silence.

'Please try and get on with him this time," says Mother. "Owen hates trouble." This is not true. Owen loves stirring things up between Mother and me, not that he needs to put much effort into it. Let's just say my relationship with the woman who apparently gave birth to me is rocky. I look at myself in the mirror. My face is puffy and my legs look heavier than usual. Either this skirt is unflattering or Mother is right, I have put on weight. This cannot be.

"Try not to mess the room up," says Mother, eyeing my two enormous suitcases. "I've only just had it decorated."

"I don't mess things up," I say coolly.

Mother clears her throat. "I'm going to work in an hour, and Owen's got a night shift, so you'll have the place to yourself. But don't use up all the hot water and. . ." She goes on about not messing up the kitchen or snooping in her room, or using her shampoo, or whatever. . .

"Whatever," I say.

Mother is the assistant manager at the one and only hotel in the village and Owen works in immigration security twenty miles away at Exeter Airport. They've been together for five years and sometimes when I visit they're all over each other, but the next time they'll barely speak. They've split up a few times but so far, unfortunately, they've always made up.

Mother looks me up and down. "You'd better change out of that skirt. You make the place look like a red-light district."

Ouch.

"Tyson needs a walk," she calls as she leaves the room. "Make yourself useful while you're here."

Tyson, Mother's dog, is eight months old and already enormous. I think he's a Dobermann crossed with something. He's got sharp teeth and a bad attitude. Personally, I think he's depressed, as he doesn't wag his tail very much. Even so, Mother likes him more than she does most people, even Owen, maybe even Devlin, my brother. Tyson has a bed in the kitchen with "poochie" written on it. He has three fluffy blankets and, at the last count, five coats for all weather variations – even more than me. Tyson has dog sunscreen for his ears, is given bottled water to drink in order to avoid the female hormones allegedly present in tap water, and is fed fresh meat from the butcher's. He is groomed once a fortnight at the pets' parlour and attends behavioural classes once a week. Mother takes him to the vet if he as much as sneezes. He has a large cardboard box filled with revolting chewed-up toys. Despite all this, he's a miserable animal, because for most of the day, whilst Mother's at work, he's shut up, howling, in the conservatory. It must drive the neighbours mad. I'm not keen on dogs, myself. I don't like anything which eats its own poo.

The door shuts and I am alone. I listen as the shower comes on, the other side of the wall. I stare at Manhattan. As I look, the black lines of the buildings merge with the grey and white sky and things go blurry. I swallow and breathe deeply and slowly. I'm not the crying type. It makes my eyes shrink and my nose swell, and I like to look my best. *There's no need to be homesick*, I tell myself. *I'm only here for a couple of weeks; then I can go home.* Just then the door swings open. Mother is wearing a fluffy white towel and nothing else. She has quite good muscle tone for an old person.

"Walk Tyson before dark," she orders. "I don't want you going out on your own at night."

"I see," I say, fiddling with an eyelash. At home I'm always out at night. I love night. I'm a night person.

"There's been a few funny types passing through," Mother says. "Tramps and gypsies and foreigners. Weirdos. This village isn't what it was." She looks at me like she expects me to sympathise.

"That sounds pretty racist," I mutter before I can stop myself. And from the look on her face, I think I have officially blown my Good Start.

One afternoon, two weeks ago and without any warning, Dad switches off the TV.

Uh oh, I think, *this is big*.

TV is on 24/7 in our house.

"Lexi, love." Dad clears his throat and rubs his cheek. The bristles crackle under his palm. He's calling me "love"; therefore he has something bad to tell me. I wait, giving him the evil eye. Not many people like my dad. He's done some dodgy stuff in the past and been in trouble with the police a few times, but says that's all behind him now. He's got a short fuse but he's stuck by Devlin and me, which is more than I can say for some people.

Dad shifts around in his chair, clears his throat. "Lexi . . . we need to talk." He looks worried but I'm intrigued. What's he done now?

"If it's about college, I'm going no matter what you say." I glare at him. "I'll earn money in the evenings."

"It's not about college, I'm proud you're going to college. Did I ever say you shouldn't go?" Dad frowns.

"You've implied it," I say. "You said when you were sixteen you were earning a wage. . ."

"Lexi," Dad cuts in. "This isn't about college. It's just that. . ."

"What?" I'm really curious now. I don't think I've ever seen Dad look so worried. He won't stop rubbing his face. He starts saying something, then changes his mind. This has to be about a woman. Maybe he's finally found a new girlfriend and he wants her to move in. . .

"I've got a proposition for you," he says.

"No," I say. I'd have to meet her first, at least.

"Ha, ha," says Dad.

"Forget it."

"You don't know what it is yet," says Dad.

"Yes I do," I say, and am surprised at the look of horror that passes over Dad's face.

"You what?"

"What's her name?" I ask, making a grab for the remote, but he holds it up out of my reach. He breathes out in relief.

"This isn't about a woman, Lexi." At this I start to get a sinking feeling. Things, for once, are going my way. I'm starting college to do A-levels in a month (psychology, communications and English) and I'm finally, definitely over my ex, Chas Parsons. And now this. Whatever it is, I don't want to know. I get up to go.

"Sit," orders Dad.

I was wrong. This isn't big, it's enormous. I sit down,

glaring at Dad and folding my arms. When he comes out with it, it's worse than I imagined.

"How would you like to stay with your mother for a few days?" he says, kneading his eye sockets so he doesn't have to look at me. My jaw drops. I shut it quickly. It's not my look.

"I wouldn't," I say.

Mother walked out on us when I was two years old and Devlin was four. We don't get on. We see each other three or four times a year and this is more than enough.

"I need to go away," says Dad, not meeting my eye.

"Fine, I can stay here," I say.

"No can do, I'm afraid," says Dad. "I'll be gone for at least three weeks. You can't be here on your own for that long."

"You said just a few days." I pick imaginary specks from my jumper. "And I wouldn't be on my own; I'd have Devlin."

But Dad goes on to tell me that he's already set some work up for Devlin with Uncle Petey in Kent. He also says that Mother has already agreed to have me.

"Lexi?"

"Where are you going?"

"I'm going to France," says Dad. "I'm doing some business with a wine merchant."

Dad buys stuff and sells it over the internet. Even so, this is all a bit fishy. For one thing, Mother and Dad aren't into cosy chats behind my back, and for another,

Devlin, a.k.a. Motormouth, has said nothing about this to me.

"Is this dodgy?" I ask.

"Of course not," says Dad, frowning.

He must think I'm stupid. "Uncle" Petey is a crook; he's a mate of Dad's from way back. I didn't even know they were still in touch. I dread to think what Devlin's getting involved in.

"Why can't I come with you?" I ask. "I've passed GCSE French."

"This is work," says Dad. "Not a bloody school trip." He's annoyed. Most people would back off at this stage. Dad's temper is legendary round here. However, I am not most people.

"You're up to something dodgy," I say. "Tell me what all this is really about."

"Lexi," says Dad. "I swear I'm not doing anything illegal." His voice breaks up and he looks away. "Quite the opposite."

I walk out of the room.

Gutted.

The Howling

People (Mother; Dad; Moz, my best mate, to name but a few) tell me that I'm very up and down. I'm a teenager, I'm supposed to have mood swings, but no one seems to take that into consideration. I get happy, I get sad, end of story. Is that so unusual? But Moz says most people operate somewhere between the two. This sounds like no-man's-land to me. I like a bit of passion and excitement in life. Though I have to admit that right at this moment, I'm pretty down. I shut myself in my white room and wait for Mother and Owen to leave. Minutes after they've gone, there's scrabbling at my door and the dog barges in. Mother has bought him a new collar; it's silver, with studs in the shape of hearts. He's about to leap on to my bed when I step in his way.

"Beat it, stink-hound."

Tyson growls, wrinkling his snout and flashing his teeth. He's got so big so quickly. Last time I saw him, he was just a mad puppy. He bounds towards me and before I can stop him, he's reared up on his hind legs and landed his paws on my shoulders. I get a waft of his hot, stale breath before I manage to push him off.

So much for the behavioural classes. He plonks himself down in the middle of the floor and begins to lick his intimate parts. "This is my room now," I say, showing him the door. "Wash your dirty dog's bottom somewhere else." To my surprise he slinks off, and a few minutes later I hear his claws on the tiles downstairs, so I decide to have a proper look round up here.

Mother and Owen keep their bedroom very tidy. It's painted red and cream with big flower prints. It looks like something out of a magazine, apart from Mother's eye mask and the earplugs she wears every night. Mother has always been obsessive about sleep. I open a cupboard and find it rammed with Mother's potions. She's got everything: expensive perfumes, packs of unopened make-up, hair dyes and treatments. I wish I could afford this stuff. Her clothes are all beautifully ironed and in the built-in wardrobes. I avoid touching Owen's things because I don't want to contaminate myself. The mirror is a good one, it makes me look thinner than the one in my room, but my hair needs a wash. . .

OUCH!

Clutching my calf, I see Tyson's hairy back shooting out the doorway. "I'll get you put down for this," I yell after him, collapsing on the bed to examine my leg. Blood beads from the skin and it hurts! I hope I don't get rabies or worms or some other revolting dog disease. I limp to the bathroom to find something antiseptic but end up getting distracted because in here the shelves are loaded with yet more beauty products. After a hot shower I'm not feeling any better because Mother's expensive shampoo has made my hair really dry. I put on my pyjamas, arm myself with a rolled-up magazine and go downstairs to make a sandwich. Tyson darts out to meet me and I raise the magazine, ready to wallop him if need be, but he scampers off to the front door.

"I'm not taking you for a walk, you big creep." Tyson wuffs at me. He kind of reminds me of someone. He's got the same bad attitude as my dad. I wonder how Dad's doing in France. He says he might even get into the wine-selling business full time after this trip. I'm not so sure. I think he's up to something, and this wine thing is just a cover. I'll find out eventually; I always do.

Tyson won't leave me alone the entire time I'm making my sandwich. Oh God. I suppose he needs a crap. I edge round him, worried he might nip me again, until I reach the front door. I hold it wide open.

"Go on, then."

Tyson streaks out of the door and flies up the path like he's after a gold rabbit. I have no wish to watch him do his business so I go back indoors and finish making my sandwich. But it's half an hour later and I'm lying on the sofa flicking through the telly channels before I remember him. I open the front door but can't see him anywhere. It's dark. All I can hear is the buzzing of the giant electricity pylon, which stands in a paddock just behind the house.

"TYSON." After a minute I nip back inside for a coat, swearing under my breath, but the only one on the hook belongs to Owen and it stinks of aftershave and sweat, so I go outside in just my pyjamas and bare feet. I walk down the garden path and look up and down the deserted street, the tarmac cold beneath my toes. Everyone's doors are shut and curtains are pulled tight, but I imagine people spying on me between the gaps. Bewlea is that sort of place. Mother's house is in the old council estate at the bottom of the village. It's the last one on the street, number fifty-eight.

"Tyson," I call lamely, hugging myself because it's chilly out here. He could have gone anywhere. I'm annoyed now. This is my first night and I've already messed up. But how was I to know the dog would run off? There's a big forest just beyond the village. It stretches for miles and miles. I hope Tyson hasn't gone there; I'll never find him. I sigh. Mother is going to go mad if he doesn't come back. She might even think I've lost him on purpose. I stare at the big full moon. Dad says people go a bit crazy on a full moon. He says women have their babies and the police put more manpower out on the streets to deal with the loonies. He says people get charged up and do crazy things.

I hear light footsteps and spin round to see a dark figure dart out from a garden and sprint down the road. There's a large dog bounding at his side.

"TYSON," I bellow, rushing out into the road. As he passes under a street light, I see a bloke with long hair belting along with what I think is my mother's dog bounding behind.

"HEY," I shout. "You've got my dog." The man glances back at me but keeps going. I hobble after them, the asphalt cutting into my feet. The dog is haring along with such obvious enjoyment it makes me think it isn't Tyson after all.

"Hey!"

The figure seems to pour over the high wall at the end of the road and the dog springs up after him. Then they've gone and I'm left looking at the empty street. I'd never catch them, even if I was wearing my trainers. That bloke ought to be in the Olympics. I stare at the spot I last saw him. He jumped over that wall no problem. So things really do happen in this deadly place after all. Thieves don't really worry me. My brother, Devlin, has a thieving habit. He's been at it since he was about seven. My feet are going numb with cold. I'd better go back. Should I, God forbid, call the police? But I'm not one hundred per cent sure that was Tyson. He was too far away to tell for sure. And there was definitely something un Tyson ish about the way he was leaping around with such dog-joy.

I wait up until Mother gets home, going out to check the front garden every ten minutes in case Tyson returns, but Mother's not back before midnight and by then I'm absolutely knackered. Mother looks surprised to find me stretched out on the sofa.

"Tyson bit me," I say before she's even taken off her jacket.

"What?"

"And I'm afraid he ran off. I've been out calling but he's been gone since seven. I'm a bit worried he's been stolen." Good. I've said it. Now the only way is up. Mother stares at me for a moment, then she does up all her jacket buttons again. She goes outside and calls for him. She's out there for twenty minutes before she returns, sadly alone.

"You NEVER let him out without a lead," she says, her eyes wide with worry.

"I'm sorry, I didn't know. I didn't want to go near him after he BIT me," I say. "Look." I show her my bite mark but she barely glances at it.

"Oh, Lexi," she says, her face crumpling up, and I feel really, really bad.

"I really think he was stolen," I say. "By a scruffy man with long hair. I saw them running down the street."

"Are you sure it was Tyson?"

"It was dark," I say. "But I think so."

"I think you're lying," says Mother, her face hardening. "I think you deliberately let him run off and all this about a thief is just to let you off the hook. . ."

"No." I try to defend myself but it's no good. She's going for me in a big way. I watch her lips moving and let her words bounce off my skin. Her lipstick is miraculously still intact after a five-hour shift. I wonder what sealer she uses? Eventually Mother stops bitching at me and goes to bed. It's late, after all, and she cannot

14

function without her nine hours of shut-eye. I drag myself up to bed after her but I can't sleep. After a while I get out of bed and go to the window. I open it and breathe in the night air and look up at the moon. I didn't mean to upset Mother. I never do, but always seem to manage it.

I hear something over the buzz and crackle of the electricity pylon. It's coming from far away, from the forest up beyond the village. It's like moaning, or wailing. The noise rises and falls with the wind and as I listen, a prickle of cold runs up my back.

It's dogs howling, a long way away. It sounds spooky and kind of sad. They must be howling at the moon. I don't blame them, really; right now I feel like howling myself.

The Forest

"I don't see why he has to take a gun." I pick at the cream satin pelmets Mother insists on having on the back of her armchairs.

"Nor do I," says Mother. "But hunting is your thing, isn't it, darling?" She gives Owen a cold smile. She's lying on the sofa, sipping green tea. She's more upbeat this morning, but she's still not impressed with me.

"Maybe I'll finally catch you a rabbit," says Owen. This is insane and we all know it. My mother would no more eat a rabbit than I would. I'm dressed in a hoody I swiped from Devlin, my jeans and my old trainers. I hope I don't bump into anyone significant.

It's eight-thirty in the morning and Owen and I have been ordered to go out and look for Tyson. Owen says we're going to start looking in Bewlea Forest. Mother said this was optimistic because the place is enormous, but Owen said we had to start somewhere. He also said he'd go on his own because I'd only be in the way (hear hear) but Mother put her foot down.

"She lost him, she can find him," she says. I wonder if she used to stand up to my dad like this? If so, no wonder they split up. Dad likes having his own way all the time. But I've noticed Owen's a bit soft where Mother is concerned.

"You look like something the cat dragged in." Mother looks me up and down as she smoothes her perfect hair with her perfect nails.

"I know," I snap. "I didn't pack my dog-hunting wardrobe."

"If you hadn't let Tyson run away, you wouldn't have needed one," she replies.

"I didn't let him run away, he was stolen," I repeat. No need to mention that I left him on his own in the garden for half an hour beforehand.

"Give the kid a break, Paula," says Owen, tying the laces on his boots. "You know it's possible." I've noticed that when Owen talks to Mother, his voice is gentler than with me.

"I heard dogs howling last night," I say. "It sounded like it came from the forest."

"That would be the hunt kennels," says Owen. I try not to look at his brown hairy calf as he folds his socks over his boots. "There's a pack of staghounds kept up at Chatterton."

"But isn't hunting banned?" I ask, feeling stupid.

Owen just grins.

"Why don't you come too?" I ask Mother, knowing she won't in a million years. Mother doesn't "do" nature.

"I've got to phone the RSPCA and the dogs' home as soon as they open," she says. "Besides, someone has to be here in case he comes home." She looks away and I get another pang of remorse. I think I saw a tear in her eye. I've never seen her cry before. I watch as Owen slings the gun behind his back. I don't know much about guns but I think it's a kind of rifle. I don't feel very happy about it. He keeps it locked in a special metal cabinet under the stairs. Myself, I think it's pretty sick to go out hunting small fluffy animals.

"Please find my dog," calls Mother as we leave.

Owen's heavy breathing fogs up the car windows in about two minutes, and although I lean as far away from him as possible, his massive hand brushes up against my leg whenever he changes gear. I hope this isn't intentional.

Bewlea (pronounced Bow-lee) is a tame little village, full of old people with big cars. There are lots of tidy front gardens and houses with flashing burglar alarms and giant plastic butterflies stuck to the walls. All the lamp posts seem to have *Neighbourhood Watch* stickers slapped on them. In all the times I have come here, I've never seen anyone my age. The village green consists of one set of goalposts and a small duck pond with no ducks. Owen stops to buy sweets from the post office store. From my vantage point I can see the tea rooms, the windows dribbling with condensation, and Friars Hotel, where Mother works. I wind down the window and read the posters on the notice board. A faded pink Post-It note, scrawled over with biro, is stuck to the cork board with a drawing pin. It's about another missing dog; a spaniel, Tess, aged six months. I wonder if *she* ever came home. There's also a poster asking people to attend a parish meeting about the future of Nyasha Agruba. Who's she? Someone has put graffiti over the poster in black pen.

SEND HER BACK

Owen pulls open his door and flings a handful of barley sugars in my lap. "Eat," he orders. "You're going to need the energy."

"No thank you," I say, putting them on the dashboard. I'd love one but I'm not eating anything Owen has given me. Also my thighs look rather on the large side, splayed out on the car seat. I zip up my hoody. It's an overcast day and looks like it might rain. I can't let my hair get wet or it will frizz up. This morning, after my shower, my hair straighteners didn't heat up properly. Nightmare! Mother said hers needed a new fuse so I couldn't use them either, so I've had to blow-dry my hair, which took me thirty minutes.

Owen chucks a big bottle of cola on the dashboard and tells me to help myself. Then he rips open the wrapper of a sweet and stuffs it into his mouth. I look out of the window as he sucks. "Relax," he slurps. "I'm not going to bite."

"Good," I mutter.

"Sometimes I think your mum loves that dog more than she loves me," he goes on, wiping his mouth. I agree but decide it's best to say nothing. "Or you," he adds nastily. He pulls out into the road without looking and a passing car honks at us. I drum my fingers on my leg.

"So how long do you think your dad is going to be away?" Owen gives my boobs a sidelong glance and has to swerve to avoid a parked car.

"Three weeks."

We drive out of Bewlea and hurl along the country lanes. I'm praying we don't meet anything coming the other way; the road isn't wide enough.

"Have a drink." Owen gestures at the bottle of cola.

I'm thirsty and decide it's better to have a swig before Owen gets his horrible mouth around it, so I reach for the bottle and unscrew the cap. I'm just putting it to my mouth when Owen swerves, and the bottle jolts out of my fingers and I am covered with sticky black liquid.

I look over at him, furious. My hoody and jeans are drenched.

"Sorry," says Owen. "I thought I saw a cat."

To my credit, I say nothing. I manage this by clamping my teeth together and counting to twenty very slowly. But inside I am seething. Did he do that deliberately? I can never tell with Owen. I don't take my hoody off, but sit there, damp and mad. It's about two or three miles before we cross a big fast road, then another mile winding uphill before we reach the forest. Owen turns up a road marked "PRIVATE". We accelerate up a hill through an avenue of big old trees. It's quite pretty but I so wish I was at home in Bexton. It feels like my life is out of control. It's bad enough coming

20

four times a year on my duty visits, but this time I don't even know how long I'm going to be stuck here.

Devlin, my brother, spends much more time with Mother than me. Though he has to be careful. Last year he got caught stamping on some cars outside Mother's house, and as he'd already been in trouble for other stuff, he ended up with an ASBO – an Anti-Social Behaviour Order – which means he's forbidden to come within five miles of Bewlea. So now Mother has to smuggle him in when she wants to see him. She doesn't appear to mind. I'm not jealous that, despite being a nutcase, he's Mother's favourite, but it would be nice if she occasionally indicated she liked me. Ever since I was tiny I had the impression she preferred it when I wasn't around. She left my dad when I was two and Devlin was four. I remember sitting on the stairs, cuddling Devlin, who was crying because Mummy wasn't there. Later, at school, I was the only kid in my class whose mum, not dad, was being chased for child-maintenance payments.

We pull into a clearing on the side of the road. Owen turns off the engine. "I walk Tyson up here sometimes," he says. "Especially when I need to get out of the house after a scrap with your mum." He looks meaningfully at me. "So maybe he's come back here on his own. There's a big badger sett he's keen on so we'll look there first." He hands me a small metal whistle. "I don't suppose this will work," he says. "But it's worth a try." I put the whistle in my hoody pocket. We get out of the car. It's not raining yet; that's something. There's some hope for my hair. I sit up on the bonnet and look gloomily around. I see nothing but tall fir trees in every direction. They grow densely in rows, their lower branches brown through lack of sunlight. I shiver.

"I've got a spare jacket in the boot," says Owen. "You'd better wear that. It's not a warm day."

I could have told him that. I dislike the idea of wearing something of Owen's, but I dislike being cold even more. Grumpily I slide off the car and rummage in the back, pulling out a rumpled red-checked lumber-jack shirt. It is so not me but I put it on and am enveloped in Owen's smell. He really should not wear so much aftershave.

"Very fetching," he says, grinning.

I say nothing. I am in a mega-strop and do not trust myself to speak.

"We'd better not split up," says Owen. "You'll only get yourself lost."

"No I won't," I say, breaking my silence at the thought of traipsing around with him. "I'm not stupid."

Owen shrugs. "OK, you look down there." He points down a track with deep grassy tractor ruts. "At the bottom there's a stream; when you reach it, come straight back. Here are the keys in case you get back before me." Owen hands them to me. The plastic fob is warm from his pocket and contains a mini photograph of Mother in a gold bikini.

"Off you go, then," Owen says, sounding amused. "And don't forget to call for him; he's not telepathic."

I wander down the track, treading carefully through the long grass. After a few minutes I double back. I have no intention of wandering around this place. I'll get my trainers soggy. There's no sign of Owen. Good. I unlock the car and get in. I put the key in the ignition and switch on the radio. When I've found a decent station I sit back in my seat and close my eyes. We don't even know that Tyson is in this wood anyway. I listen to the radio for ages but it makes me feel sad, I don't know why. I'm just beginning to feel guilty about not looking for Tyson when I realize I need a wee. I'm going to have to go behind a bush, but it's so undignified. I'm not a hedge monkey who likes climbing trees and making coffee from dandelions. The closest I want to get to nature is with my herbal shampoo. I select a tree a little way away from the car and do my business as quickly as possible, hoping Owen isn't spying on me. But the forest is still and quiet. I think I'm safe. As I stand up to do up my jeans I find something hard in my pocket. It's the dog whistle. I wipe it on my jeans, then, just for the hell of it, give a long blow. I hear nothing, like I'm supposed to. I give it another go, just in case Tyson decides to come bounding out of the undergrowth. Then we can all go home and Mother will be pleased with me for a change.

I wander a little way back down the track. Even if I don't find the dog, I could do with burning off a few calories, and I suppose it's quite chilled here. I've got mud on the hem of my jeans. I hope it doesn't stain. A smaller path, shot with gold and pink flowers, branches off the main track, and I decide to investigate. Pretty soon the fir trees thin out and the path broadens. I walk into a large clearing with five small silvery trees growing in the middle. Even I think this place is pretty. I pick a bit of bright green moss off a tree trunk and sniff the earthy smell. Look at me! I'll be collecting leaves for a collage next.

I hear something growling behind me.

"Tyson?"

A large dog crouches about three metres away from me, staring at me with mad glittering eyes. I take in a sharp breath and freeze. It's not Tyson. I step back very slowly in case any sudden moves might set it off. It looks like a cross between an Alsatian and a small horse. I'd guess it's mostly white, with a few brown patches, but its legs and back are caked in mud. It's got a bramble wrapped up in its tail. It's a monster.

"Hello, doggy," I say in a friendly dog-loving voice, trying not to show my fear. Isn't that what you're supposed to do in these situations? Don't let them know you're frightened? The dog growls again, showing me its big yellow teeth and black-edged tongue. It's dead skinny and looks hungry. I keep backing away, speaking in my wheedling voice. "Good dog, good doggie." Where the hell is this thing's owner, or is it a stray? I can't believe how big it is. I'm thinking the growling is beginning to ease off when it darts forward, barking right in my face. I can't hide my fear now. I break and run.

"Help!" I yell. Oh my God – it's got the heel of my shoe in its teeth. I trip and kick out, catching it in the side of its horrible head. The animal grunts and I pick myself up and run on and on. I run through the trees, pushing through brambles and bracken, and I'm getting scratched to pieces but this can't be as bad as being eaten alive.

"Help," I scream. "Help, help, bloody help!" If I can get back to the car, I could shut myself in. But the dog's right behind me, barking madly. It keeps jumping up and trying to nip me. I decide to somehow try and circle round the trees back to the car, but before I can do this I spot a second dog pelting through the trees towards me. This one is black and white and smaller than the first, but has the same mad, hungry look. It's a kind of collie. Jesus, it's coming for me. I duck sideways, but it manages to nip my thigh.

"What did I do to you?" I scream as sharp pain races up my leg. I head for a dense clump of trees; one of them looks maybe climbable. But the collie is somehow right in front of me, oh God it's like it's *herding* me! So I have to change direction and run blindly on. I skid to a halt. I've come into a kind of small quarry. The slopes are too steep for me to climb, so I'm cornered. The collie flies in and before I know it, it's got the cuff of Owen's lumberjack shirt and is pulling and growling and staring at me. I slip the top off and the dog shakes it like a rat before dropping it and turning back to me, a string of drool falling from its jaws. The monster dog comes forward to join him. They're edging closer, getting ready for the kill.

Lost

I lash out with my foot and hit the collie on the muzzle. He yelps and springs back and I notice the tatty remains of a collar round his neck. Monster dog creeps towards me, its back quivering and foam flecking its mouth. I shut my eyes and smell something rank, like old milk, and open them again. The monster dog is directly in front of me. I'm tense with fear and going hot and cold.

I'm bloody not going to be eaten by these things.

"Bugger off," I scream, and wallop him hard on the head with my fist. He snaps at the air and falls back. It gives me a few moments to scour the slope on my left. There's a snapped-off branch lying in the moss. It will have to do. "Just clear off," I scream, grabbing the branch. Adrenaline floods my body. I'm not scared any more. I'm mad. I run at the monster, screaming and waving my stick. He's not giving up easily, though. He runs in and nips the back of my elbow, so I bring the stick down hard on his back. It snaps in two and the dog whines and shrinks away, slathering and snapping his jaws like he's having a fit. I didn't think rabies existed in this country, but these dogs are absolutely crazy.

"Go," I yell, and advance again. This time I'm holding a stone in my hand. I'm going to smash it down on his bloody head, I'm going to. . .

But both dogs prick up their ears and look round like they've heard something. Then I hear a soft whistle. Somebody is calling them off. The monster gives me one last growl, and then they are gone, pelting off between the trees. I stare after them, clutching my stone, my heart thumping.

"Hello?" I call. "Hello? Your dogs just attacked me." There's no reply. The forest is quiet. Even the birds have stopped singing. All I hear is the whisper of the wind through the trees and a sheep bleating a long way away. Then I realize I don't know how to get back to the car.

Here's how it is. I'm lost, hungry and tired. Owen's shirt was ripped and covered in dog spit, so I left it behind, and now I'm shivering. I've been shouting for Owen for hours. I'm alone in this wood apart from those hideous dogs, which I imagine are lurking somewhere nearby. I can't find the car; I can't find the road. I'm wandering around in circles. It all looks the same to me. What's the use of places like this? If I had my way we'd chop down all the bloody trees and make nice houses and streets and bring civilization to this vile place.

I can't believe I've got myself lost in Bewlea Forest. If I walk in a straight line, I will get out. That's logic. But

I'm not getting anywhere. Every rustle, every crackle I hear freaks me out, making me think the dogs are back. It would be too embarrassing to be eaten alive. Imagine what the kids at school would say. They'd kill themselves laughing. My hand throbs and my leg is stinging. Thankfully my face didn't get bitten. I would hate to have a scar.

"Owen, where are you?" I yell half-heartedly, paranoid the dogs will hear me and come running back to finish me off. I'm checking behind me when my feet plunge into something wet and cold. I'm knee-deep in a brown puddle and I grab at a clump of reeds to haul myself out, during which my trainer comes off and I have to pull it out of the mud. I sit on a prickly bank and try to clean my shoe on the grass but it doesn't make much difference. Reluctantly I put the filthy thing back on my foot. I check my mobile signal again. Nope. Still nothing. I look up at a load of birds circling high above the trees.

I can't believe this is happening to me. I shouldn't be here. I should be hanging out in town with Moz and Debs. Or Chas. No, not Chas. He's my ex. We split up about three months ago. He was never right for me. I always knew that but I can't resist a pretty face. Besides, he made me laugh, and he thought I was God's gift. This is a fatal combination for me. Anyway, he's history now. This is sad, especially as I don't have a replacement yet. Chas still sends me the odd text.

*

Stl Luv Ya Lex

Or

Missin' U beautiful

I wish he was here now.

I try to think clearly about what I should do next, but it's hard because I'm so thirsty. I'd do anything for a Coke. I'd take on a pack of dogs. According to my watch, it's two o'clock. I haven't seen Owen for nearly five hours. Surely he's looking for me? He could shoot the dogs with his rifle if they attack him. But I can't help thinking he'll have given up by now and gone home for a nice cup of tea. Will Mother eventually call the police? She might think I've legged it back to Bexton and might not bother to raise the alarm. She'll be at work now anyway. She won't waste her time sending out the search helicopters. It's not like it's Devlin who's missing. I wonder again why she's so crazy about him. He was an über-hyperactive kid and no one could control him. I remember Dad thumping Devlin and shouting, "You (*wallop*) do not (*wallop*) beat up (*wallop*) little kids. . ."

My brother has no issue with robbing people, or nicking cars, or just about anything. But Mother talks of him like he's this sweet little boy. Devlin was never that. He even got chucked out of nursery for attacking other kids. Mother said it was a phase, but it's a bloody long one. He hardly ever went to school and now he's a real loser, in and out of prison and out of control.

I find a little stream and rinse my bitten hand. The

water doesn't look too dirty. I'm so thirsty I can't resist tasting some. It's cold and delicious. I scoop handful after handful into my mouth, like I'm a kid stuffing chocolate. I look around; I don't seem to be under imminent canine attack, so I take off my jeans and examine my war wounds. I've got a bite on the back of my thigh and another on my calf. The one on my thigh is the sorest and the blood has soaked into my jeans. I don't like seeing blood; my own is just about bearable but other people's makes me retch. I splash a little water on to the bites. River water has got to be cleaner than dog spit. I pull my jeans back on. Dad said he was going to call me today; I bet I've missed him now.

I can hear something familiar, a buzzing sound. It takes me a few seconds to work out what it is. It's the sound of an electricity pylon. I walk in the direction of the sound, looking up, and sure enough, I soon see the top of a pylon through the trees. I wonder if it is joined to the one above Mother's house? If so, all I have to do is follow the wires and I'll end up in my own back garden. The trees are thinning and I can see a big clearing just ahead. I step out into a kind of green road. It's as if someone has cleared out all the trees in a strip the width of a motorway, which stretches as far as I can see. A row of pylons march away through the centre of the strip. I turn and look in the other direction and catch sight of a chimney in the distance. Yes! A building! Civilization! I walk under the crackling electricity wires in the direction of the chimney. I panic a bit when the ground drops away and I lose sight of it, but I've got the pylons to guide me, and sure enough, a few minutes later, the chimney reappears.

It's made of red brick and looks enormous, like something you'd normally find pumping out smoke above a factory roof. As I get closer I see more chimneys and the dark, pointed roofs of what must be an absolutely massive building, bang in the middle of the forest. The trees thin out and I walk under the wires to a high fence. I press my face against the cold metal links and look at a kind of mansion, with chimneys and steps and outbuildings and a clock tower. All the ground-floor windows are boarded up and huge chunks of plaster and cement have fallen off the walls. Trails of ivy hang down from the roof and there are large cracks in the rendering. It doesn't look as if anybody has lived there for some time. I walk round the fence, looking for some way to get in. Eventually I find a hole and squeeze through. Devlin's hoody rips as it catches on the metal. I step out into the long grass, threaded with brambles and bits of trees. I pass a life-sized statue that's choked with ivy and dirt. It's a woman in a long dress, holding out her palms like she's trying to explain something. Her nose has weathered away. Just looking at her makes me feel sad; I don't know why. But I've got more important things to do than look at statues – like getting out of this forest. Close up, the house looks even more derelict. There's graffiti up the walls and broken roof tiles litter the grass.

Even so, the size of the place is still impressive; it must have been pretty grand once. Maybe it was a big public school or something. I don't understand why some developer hasn't snapped it up and turned it into flats; it could be amazing. I bet there's fantastic views from the upper floors and it would be an exciting and kooky place to live.

There's a small stone chapel behind some trees. The windows are boarded up and the front door is closed. I see a couple of gravestones round the side. I don't think there's been a vicar in there for some time!

I check my mobile signal again. Nothing. It must be because I'm so high up and there are no mobile masts around. Or maybe the trees or the electricity pylons deaden the reception. I don't know, I'm no scientist. My stomach rumbles, but remembering my massive thighs on the car seat, I decide a bit of hunger won't do me any harm. College starts soon and I don't want to look like a sow.

To my left there's a single-storey shed. The nettles almost reach the roof. Beyond that is what looks like a normal small house, except all the glass in the windows is broken and there's a huge board over the front door. There's a tree with purple flowers growing out of the chimney. A pigeon sits pecking at something on the roof. There's something glinting behind the nettles. The light is playing off it in a weird way. It's a mirror leaning against the wall. I get up and wander over for a quick check but I get a nasty shock. My hair is stuffed up with twigs and bark, and looks like I've been back-combing it. My face is pale and smudged with dirt, all my make-up seems to have come off, and I look about twelve years old. I pat down my hair, and spit on my finger to remove the worst of the grime from my face. When I'm finished I kid myself that I look at least a little bit better. As far as I can tell, there's no one here to see me, but I don't like looking a state. I'm busy working on my face when, in the mirror, I see something move in one of the upper windows of the main house. I turn to have a proper look, but everything is still. Now I'm feeling uneasy. Was that a trick of the light, or am I being watched? I brazen it out.

"Hello," I yell. "Anybody there?"

Nothing.

Someone must look after this place. Maybe there's a caretaker up there. But I don't like to shout again.

I make my way silently back to the main house and stand on my tiptoes to peer through a crack in the boarded-up window. It's too dark to see anything. All I hear is the cooing of pigeons. What is this place? Rounding a corner I find another vast wing where the windows are blackened and the roof has collapsed. I step over a burned-black beam, half buried in the grass. There must have been a big fire here at one time, but it didn't spread to the whole building. I peer through an open doorway into a space full of collapsed beams and burned furniture. Scorch marks run up the walls. I can see through the ceiling and roof right up to the sky.

I continue round the outside until I reach what I decide must be the front. There's a weed-choked courtyard area, with a drive leading off through a gate in the surrounding fence. Big stone steps lead up to a massive set of wooden doors, studded with metal and covered with graffiti. Heavy chains, secured with three industrial padlocks, criss-cross from frame to frame. Something tells me I'm not about to find a friendly caretaker who'll ring me a taxi, but there must be a phone inside, surely? I need to find some way of getting in.

A window near the front steps looks promising. The board has been pulled off and all the glass has been punched in. I hesitate. Maybe I should walk down the drive until I reach the main road. There must be mobile reception down there. This place is well spooky and I'd quite like to be on my way. But what if the dogs attack me again? I'm feeling really shivery. I don't know if I'm strong enough to fend them off this time.

A spatter of rain hits my shoulder.

That's it. I'm not having my hair ruined, especially considering my straighteners are broken.

I climb up to the window ledge and ease myself through slowly to avoid shredding myself on the remaining jags of glass. I lower myself into the darkness, stretching my toes to find the floor. Where is it? It must be lower than the ground outside. How can that be possible? I can't see much. My eyes haven't adjusted to the gloom. When I finally touch the ground it feels squidgy, like walking on a wet carpet. It's cold in here, and still. Like nothing has disturbed the air for a very long time. I wrinkle my nose. There's also an almighty pong of something dead. I look down through the gloom and see a rotting pigeon, crawling with maggots. I step away to avoid it and the evil bacteria that is going to infect my already-infected dog bites and give me blood poisoning and send me to an early grave before I've had time to do anything with my life.

Now I can see I'm in a kind of hallway, so big and wide you could have a five-a-side game of football in here. A frantic flapping makes me jump as a pigeon flutters around in the ceiling, which curves up high above my head. There's a faint light coming from the end of the corridor. I make out some broken chairs and lots and lots of broken glass on the floor. Maybe this wasn't such a good idea.

The air is chilled in here. It's like the whole place is dead. And for all I know, those dogs could have found another way in, and might be watching me with their infrared eyes, sniffing the bloodstains on my trousers. Or maybe there are mad crazy people here waiting for a nice young girl to stumble in and be murdered.

There's a steady drip, drip sound, like water falling into a deep well. I know I'm not supposed to be here. I feel seriously menaced.

Get a grip, I tell myself. But I can't. This is like some dodgy 18-rated film where something stumbles out of the darkness and kills me in a horrible way. I have to get out. Now. I take a step back to work out how I'm going to climb back up to the window ledge but lose my balance, as my foot keeps going down through the soft, rotten wood.

Suddenly, horrifyingly fast, all of me is falling through the floor; I fling out my arms but I can't save myself. I topple into darkness and there's a second of silence – then I splash into something and a shocking wave of cold engulfs me as I am immersed in freezing water. I lash out in terror, but I'm sinking into darkness. I've fallen through the floor into deep black water and I want to scream in horror but I can't breathe and I don't know which is the way to the surface. It's too cold. I can't see anything. I need to breathe. . .

The Cellar

I'm floundering and thrashing in this pit of freezing, stinking water and I can't get out. My teeth are chattering like mad, I'm colder than I've ever been in my life and I'm scared, so scared. I'm trying not to panic but it's very hard. Logically, no one is going to find me. Why should they? I just want to scream and cry but that will waste my energy. Unless someone finds me soon, this is it; I've had it. Grey light penetrates down from the hallway above, enough for me to see I'm in a huge cavernous cellar. I'm swimming in a soup of broken wood and sodden feathers and bits of floating furniture. My clothes are heavy with water, dragging on my tired body. I don't know long I'll be able to tread water; maybe a few hours? My feeble little whimpers echo off the walls. Water drips from the rafters above, landing on my face. I'm so cold. It's August but I feel like I've been plunged in the Arctic Ocean and I'm trapped under the ice. Only this is worse because it's dirty and dark. I'd prefer to drown somewhere beautiful. I knew I shouldn't have come to stay with Mother. I've been in her care less than twenty-four hours and now look at me. This time yesterday I was still packing. Dad was getting annoyed because I was taking so long, and I was livid because I didn't believe a word he'd been telling me about why I needed to leave home.

My fingers brush something soft and slimy floating in the water. A vile stench fills the air and I gag as the bloated body of a dead rat bobs into me. I splash at the water, trying to get it to go away, but it keeps floating back. The white tail, swollen and stinking, rolls through the water and strokes my face. I bat it away, trying not to be sick. Madly, I paddle towards the nearest wall, shoving debris aside with my elbows. The wall is made of sheer brick and I can't get a grip anywhere. I don't know how I'm going to survive this. I'm sinking into darkness and cold. I've been shouting but my voice is getting hoarse. No one is going to find me.

No. I can't go out without a fight. I turn over to my back and scull through the darkness until my head bumps a beam floating just below the surface. I flop my arms over it and the beam takes my weight, holding me up in the water. A new wave of fatigue comes over me as I hang there. I try not to think about the darkness beneath me. There's a massive archway in one of the cellar walls. Tightly gripping my beam, I kick out for it and swim right under into the next dark space. I look up and see the light coming through the floorboards. The pigeon is flapping far, far above in the roof space.

"Help!" I scream at it. "Bloody help me."

I kick on through the darkness. Oh man, what's that? There's a greyish rounded object floating a little way off.

It looks like a head! I can see the neck and shoulders. I stare in shock, not wanting to believe what I'm seeing. The water swirls round it and eventually I realize I'm looking at the remains of a dressmaker's dummy. I dog-paddle on but I'm feeling pretty hopeless. There must be miles of cellars. I'll go round and round in circles, getting more exhausted.

"HELP," I scream. I sound like a crazy banshee. Then I think I see a rat swimming in the water, but it's nothing, just a bit of wood.

Oh God, I'm so frightened that I'm not going to make it out. The fear is awful; it makes me want to stop trying. Then I have the completely irrational thought that the only photograph Mother has of me was taken when I was ten years old, and I've got a fringe and my teeth are too big for my face. If I get reported as missing, that photograph might be broadcast on telly.

I kick on, shivering and trembling. I'm not going to give up. Not quite yet, though it is tempting just to hang on my beam, suspended in the water, and let the cold work its way deeper and deeper into me.

Something scrabbles in the floorboards above and showers of dust and dirt fall into my hair.

"Help," I choke, and see movement in the light-hole directly above me. The sound of growling filters down into my cold ears and I groan.

The dogs have come back.

"Come and get me then!" I scream. This makes them crazy with excitement and the barking is deafening.

Maybe they'll leap in and drown themselves.

I ought to kick on, swimming through the underground until I find a way out. But I'm so tired . . . so tired . . . I just want to sleep for ever. My legs have gone numb. I'm not sure if I'm even kicking them much any more. I'm just clinging to my beam and it's getting harder and harder to do this. I'm scared that I'll lose my grip and I'll sink into oblivion and I'll end up as bloated and disgusting as that dead rat. Deep cold is creeping up my waist. Maybe once it reaches my heart . . . I'll die. I'm frightened and I can't help the tears dribbling down my face. I can't get a grip. No one is going to come. Dad isn't going to miraculously appear. Nor is Owen; he'll have gone home hours ago. There is no caretaker. I'm lost. I think of Moz. I even think of bloody Chas. Sobbing, I force myself to kick my legs and make for another wall. My movements make the dogs break into a fresh volley of barking.

"Oh shut up!" I scream in annoyance. My fingertips touch cold bricks. I feel my way along the wall, searching for a handhold or anything that might help. I have to keep going even though any movement is getting painful. My arms are rubbing raw on the beam and I need the loo. I hold it in for a few minutes before I realize there is no point, and when I wee myself I feel a few seconds of warmth before the cold bites back.

The dogs stop barking and I look up, expecting to see they've gone. I blink at a silhouette in the circle of light.

41

This time, there really is somebody up there.

"Help," I scream. "Down here! Help!" It's like all my fear is in my scream. "Down here, down here." I'm flooded with energy; it feels like my body is reconnecting with itself and coming back to life. I'm going to get out of here! But then I blink and see only a void. Whatever it was up there has gone.

"COME BACK," I wail. I wait a few seconds, but there's nothing. A sob finds its way out of me. "Get a grip," I tell myself, biting back another scream. My neck aches with the strain of looking up. "HELP." A face peers at me through the hole. I see his eyes glinting through his dark shaggy hair.

"OK," he says. And then he's gone.

I wait, treading water, breathing. I have the awful thought that this is some crazy who lives here who has no intention of rescuing me. He looked rough. And why didn't he say something like, "Don't worry, I'm going to get help." Why just "OK"?

I lose it then. I scream and scream until I can't scream any more because I know he's not coming back. I'm hysterical. I'm lost in my fear. I can't help myself any more. I feel my whole body stiffen in a cramp and I go under, the muscles in my legs locked in pain. I sink and the cold engulfs me. I flail my arms, but I can't use my legs. As I fight to get back to the surface, I'm aware of something splashing down into the water and hitting my head. For a moment I think the crazy must be throwing stones at me. But there's something dangling next to my face.

It's a rope. I grab it and wrap it round my wrist. The face reappears in the light and I wait for the muscles in my legs to unlock before I try to move. When the pain eases off, I grasp the rope. I heave myself up, hand over hand, but I can't lift myself out of the water.

"Can't do it," I gasp after a few attempts. There's no reply from above. I start to wrap the rope round my waist. This way I won't sink if the cramp comes back. But the rope abruptly yanks out of my hands.

"What are you doing?" I yell as the rope flies up out of the water and through the air. I hear feet moving over the floorboards, then nothing. I'm alone again.

"Get help," I yell hoarsely. "Phone 999." He must be a nutter, or a junkie or something. Maybe he needs very clear instructions. "GET SOMEONE HERE NOW." He has to come back. He will come back. He came back before. I swim back to my beam and drape my arms over it, pressing my cheek into the wet wood.

I don't know how long it is before another fall of dust settles into the water and I hear footsteps treading cautiously overhead.

"Please help me," I gasp. The rope splashes on the water and I grab it. I'm not letting go this time. The rope has been knotted and looped and I see wood wound into it. He's made me a ladder. Now all I have to do is climb up, but I feel weak down to my bones. I'm so tired and cold. I put my hand on a log and try to haul my foot up into a loop under the water. I keep missing, but eventually get a toehold. The water sucks at me like it doesn't want to let me go, and my arms feel like they're being pulled out of their sockets. I wrench myself out of the water, moaning with effort, my breath clouding into the air. I find the next toehold and move my hands up off the log to a knot higher up. I shut my eyes and take a deep breath. I'm going to save myself.

Climbing up a rope is hard work but I have no choice; I have to go on. My palms are burning and my legs are shaking, but I slowly, slowly creep up the rope. I'm spinning round and round in the air like a big, dead spider, but I keep going up, up, up and finally I touch the floorboards and everything hurts but there's a hand grabbing my wrist and hauling me up and dragging me on to a row of planks. I'm vaguely aware of a man's face but everything is blurry, like a snowstorm on the telly. Then my head swims and everything is spinning and I hear a thud as my head falls back on to the floor.

Nyasha

I open my eyes. I'm lying on my back under a tree. Since I've been in the house, it's stopped raining and the sky has cleared. I watch the orangey sunset light playing in the leaves. I stretch and a sharp pain shoots up my leg. I groan and turn over. Everything hurts: my back, my legs, my arms, my arm sockets, my neck, my eyes, everything. And I have a headache thumping my skull. But I'm alive. And I've never truly appreciated before now how lovely it is to be warm. I'm wrapped in a massive quilt, a patchwork of colours and patterns. This is mad. I feel like I'm in a fairy story. I look at my arms and notice they're clean, so someone must have washed me. I heave myself up into a sitting position and a wave of nausea rushes over me just as I realize I am wearing my knickers and bra but nothing else. My stomach heaves and I turn and retch and puke. When I've finished I roll away, my throat burning.

I spy my clothes hanging on a bush. They look like they've been rinsed. I peer round, looking for my rescuer, but I'm alone on the edge of the forest. I can see the fence and beyond that a vast wall which may or may not be the back of the house. I reach for my clothes but they're still damp.

"Hello," I call croakily, expecting my new best friend to turn up any minute with a cup of tea. If he's managed to produce a patchwork quilt, surely he can find a cup of tea? Or water? That's what I want. I'm so thirsty. I spot a plastic water bottle at the bottom of the clothes bush. Next to this are my shoes and an apple. I scramble out of the quilt and vomit again. Then again, and again, and my whole body aches, even my eyelids, and I go hot and cold. When it's over I crawl back into the quilt and shut my eyes.

When I can think again, I wonder about the bloke. He must have gone to get help. But where's his car? Couldn't he just drive me straight home, or to hospital? Maybe he was a walker, and didn't want to wait for me to come round before he went for help. But where'd he get the quilt? Something around here smells bad. I move away from my puke and prop myself against the trunk of the tree, but I can still smell it. Eventually I work out it's the quilt, but I haven't got anything else to wear. Oh, I so want a bath and to go to bed! Judging by the light, or rather the lack of it, it must be gone nine. I get up. I'm a bit wobbly and the bites in my thigh and hands are throbbing. My trainers are sitting close by. They've been cleaned and stuffed with dry grass. I pull them on, and wrap the quilt tightly around me.

I pick up my damp clothes and tuck them under my arm. I don't think my rescuer is coming back. My shoes squelch as I pick through the trees to the fence surrounding the house. I'm not going near the building.

If I get too close it will skewer me with glass, or a roof tile will fall on my head. Or those bloody dogs will leap out of the shadows and tear me apart. Or I'll fall down a manhole. Or something. The place is bad. It has already tried to kill me once and I'm not going to give it another opportunity.

"Where are you?" I say out loud as a soft breeze lifts my hair from my neck and makes me shiver. I follow the fence round to the main gates and read the signs.

TRESPASSERS WILL BE PROSECUTED
DANGER FALLING MASONRY
WARNING GUARD DOGS ON PATROL

"Bit bloody late for that," I mutter.

I walk away down the road in the half-light, dragging the quilt, my wet trainers slapping over the ground. I feel hollow inside and light-headed. The headache has subsided to a kind of drone. I feel a bit pissed, to be honest. If the dogs came out now I'd just laugh at them. I notice I am developing a blister on my heel from the wet shoes but decide not to let it bother me. The road curves downhill. Clumps of grass break through the tarmac. My whole leg is hurting now, and each step jars the bite wound. I swear it's swelled up; my ankle looks much thicker than usual. I hope it goes down again. I couldn't stand being like the old women whose legs spill down the outside of their slippers.

I've been walking for ever. And now I'm worried I've somehow taken the wrong turning and I'm just getting deeper into the forest. I step over a rotten branch, fallen into the road. Nobody has driven up here for months. And of course I'm curious about who saved me, and who the dogs belong to, but all I can properly think about is the deep, hot bath I'm going to have if and when I get back to Mother's house.

It's nearly dark, and I'm unhappily contemplating whether or not I might have to spend the night here, when I hear the hum of an engine and see blue lights flickering against the trees. As the road bends, I find a clearing filled with people and flashing lights. There's an ambulance too. A police dog spies me and starts barking. I give it the V sign. There's about five coppers all poring over a map. They don't notice me walking up to them.

"Can I have a lift?" I tap a woman on the shoulder and she gives a little shriek.

Then I see Owen, parked a little way off, sitting in his car and gabbling away into his phone.

"Hey!" I head towards him. "Over here!" But before I can get any further, the policewoman has grabbed my arm.

"Lexi Juby?" she asks.

"When I last looked," I reply. I don't especially like the police. There have been one or two Unfortunate Incidents in my past. However, I smooth my hair as a policeman approaches. He's tall, dark and pretty hot. I

48

must look like a right tart in this manky old bedspread.

"We've found her," announces the policewoman.

I must be pretty thick not to have realized before, but it dawns on me that this little show is all for my benefit. "No," I smile weakly at the hot cop, "I found you."

After all the fuss in the forest, I think it's credible that the news cameras and photographers at the hospital gates are waiting for me to show up. I sit in the ambulance, wondering if I'm going to be sick again, and stare out the window at the crowd. Wow! I was only gone for about ten hours. It looks like I'm going to be on TV. I check my reflection in the ambulance window and nearly scream. I look like my ugly twin and my make-up has come off. I bite my lips to give them some colour and work at my hair. I wonder if the female paramedic has some lippy.

"They're not here for you," she says, watching me. I spot some placards in the crowd.

NYASHA'S HOME = CHARLTON, UK
NYASHA BELONGS HERE
SUPPORT NYASHA AGRUBA

The ambulance pulls into a bay and stops. The paramedic fills in her notes, and as I look out the window, a small woman comes down the steps of the hospital, wrapped in a purple blanket and surrounded by people and

49

flashing lights. She's ushered into a taxi and driven away.

"Who's that?" I ask.

"Nyasha Agruba," says the paramedic, without looking up. "She's a failed asylum seeker and due to be deported next month. She's lived here for five years. Her son is settled in primary school here. She collapsed last night at a community meeting. There's a public outcry. Don't you ever watch the news?"

"I'm sixteen," I say. "I've got better things to do." Then I'm sick all over the ambulance floor.

The Announcement

Mother chooses to drop her bombshell on the way home from hospital. I get discharged after three nights, even though my stomach isn't right and my joints still ache like I'm an old woman. I'm sitting in the back of Owen's car, fingering my cheek, worrying my skin is ruined because I have applied no moisturizer for three whole days. On the first day in hospital Mother bought me some clothes from home to wear, but forgot any beauty products. She picked out my black jeans and a fairly decent top, so at least I don't look completely awful. Mother said she'd told the hospital to incinerate my other clothes. I made out I was mad even though I secretly agreed with her. They were disgusting.

In hospital I was sick for the first twenty-four hours, puking my guts out. I was so glad I was in my own room; I'd have died if anyone had seen me in that state. The nurses said I was very lucky my wounds weren't infected. I tried to tell them it was because someone had washed them for me, but they were too busy jabbing me with tetanus injections and dripping saline fluid into my arm so I didn't dry up like a corpse.

51

When Mother arrived at the hospital the first evening she looked tired under all her make-up. Along with the clothes, she'd bought me a pile of fashion magazines.

Aha, I thought. Has the ice queen actually been *worried* about me?

"Are you OK?" she asked, and actually kissed my cheek.

"Yes," I said, wondering if my cheek was going to shrivel up. She handed me my toothbrush and pyjamas.

"What were you doing up there in the first place?" she said. "You could have died! I can't believe you were so stupid. Everyone knows Beacon House Hospital is a death trap."

"Well I didn't." I felt myself boil up into a rage. "I was looking for your bloody dog, and if you'd bothered to look for him yourself, I wouldn't be here now."

"Right," said Mother, tight-lipped, and stared out of the window. That was definitely the wrong thing to say. Tyson hasn't come back yet. I don't think there's going to be any more kisses.

On day two, a woman copper came on to the ward to talk to me. She was at least fifty and her blouse was too small. She had sweat patches under her arms. When I told her about my mystery rescuer she made some notes in her pad, then went on and on about trespassing and breaking and entering. I think she thought I was just a mad teenager up to no good. She did mention that she'd run into my brother a few times. It's hard being a Juby;

52

everyone thinks I'm bound to be as bad as the rest of my family. Eventually she left me alone.

Now I hunch in the back seat of the car, trying not to look at Owen's hairy neck straining against his collar.

"Lexi, we've got something to tell you that might cheer you up," says Mother. Maybe she's going to tell me how terrified she was when I was missing and how much she loves me. I watch Owen's fat thumbs tapping the steering wheel.

"Owen has asked me to marry him."

What?

"Ha, ha," I say. "As if." After Dad, Mother swore she'd never marry again. There's a bit of a silence, in which a seed of doubt begins to grow in me. She couldn't, she wouldn't, would she?

"I said yes," says Mother.

I pretend to be very interested in the dressing on my hand. Then my mouth feels furry and I think I'm going to be sick again. I feel like crying. I've just been through a nightmare, and now this.

"We're doing it soon," says Mother. "Next month, as a matter of fact, before I change my mind, ha, ha." She looks at Owen.

"Ha ha," he says, unimpressed.

I think there's something going on here.

"So," says Mother lightly. "Have we taken your mind off things? We've actually been planning the wedding for some time already, but wanted to wait for the right moment to tell you."

"Congratulations," I say quietly. "What a catch."

I've always secretly hoped that one day, me and Mother would get on better. Moz and her mum, Sally, are almost like mates; they go shopping together, watch films together and just seem to enjoy each other's company. There's no way Mother and I will ever get close like that if she's married to Owen. He brings out the worst in me. I can't help turning into a grouchy she-devil when he's around. Mind you, even before Owen was on the scene, Mother and I had our differences. I was a funny little kid and I thought I'd be somehow disloyal to Dad if Mother and I had a half-decent time together. Now I'd quite like us to get on, but we just seem to wind each other up, all the time.

"Devlin can give me away," says Mother. "I've got him a suit."

I suppress a snort of hysterical laughter. He'll go insane. Mother gives me a meaningful look in the lipstick mirror.

"Don't even think about asking me to be a bridesmaid," I say without thinking.

"I wasn't," says Mother. "I knew you'd say no."

Ouch! Not that I'd want to be dressed up in frills and Lord knows what. But it would have been nice to have been asked. I am her daughter, after all.

"I've already got a bridesmaid," says Mother.

"Who?"

"Celia Parker," says Mother. Now I understand why Mother doesn't want me as bridesmaid. She knows I'd upstage her. Celia Parker couldn't upstage a hippo. She's dead old – at least forty – weighs twenty-three stone and is waiting for a cap for one of her front teeth.

When we get back I go straight up to my room and bang the door.

A couple of days after I come "home", I'm locked in the bathroom looking at myself in the mirror. My chin still has a scratch on it and I have huge bags under my eyes. I'm pale and my hair is lank. I look old. I keep phoning Dad; I need to talk to him about what happened, but he isn't answering his mobile, and our home phone just beeps. Mother says she's sure he'll call very soon but I worry something has happened to him and nobody is telling me. Mother said she contacted him just after I was brought into hospital, so he knows all about it. So why hasn't he called? I don't understand. I shut my eyes and at once I'm back in that cellar, struggling and thrashing in the black water. My chest starts to feel tight and I open my eyes.

"Cool it," I tell my reflection, and after a few minutes, my chest feels normal again. I'm sure I've got post-traumatic stress syndrome or something. I haven't slept well. I've had bad dreams about drowning. I wake up replaying what happened to me over and over again. I don't know what's the matter with me. No one in my family suffers from nerves; if anything, we suffer from a lack of them. I was never afraid of monsters under the bed. Even as a little kid I knew I could just chase them away.

Real monsters, like Owen, are far scarier. Through the floorboards I hear him laughing at the TV. I can't imagine introducing him to my mates as my stepdad; it's too freaky. Celia, Mother's chief bridesmaid, was round here yesterday and she goes, "Oh, I hear you had a little accident, Lexi?" And I said, "It wasn't a little accident; I nearly died." Then Celia just giggled nervously and started a debate with Mother about whether they should have gold or silver balloons for the wedding breakfast. That's how much people care about me round here.

I hate being this cross and miserable. I need to cheer up. I need to think about the good things, like, like. . . I'll think of something.

You only live once, so you may as well be beautiful, even if your life is falling apart. The mirror is telling me I have work to do. After washing, there's hair removal, with razors, sticky strips, and cream, depending on the body part. Next, my hair has to be shampooed, then conditioned (I'm doing a deep condition this morning. I have to leave on the gunk for twenty minutes with a plastic bag on my head). During this time I exfoliate my skin with foaming scrub, especially the backs of my arms, knees and feet. (I scrub and tone my face with special face products.) I wash out the hair conditioner and step out of the shower. I wrap myself in towels,

then floss and brush my teeth with whitening paste. Then I moisturize my whole body, with my feet, my eye area and my face all having their own specialized moisturizers. Then I move out of the bathroom to tackle my hair. It takes twenty minutes to blow-dry. When my hair is done, I apply some hand cream and spray myself with a light summery perfume.

Nobody knows who the bloke was who rescued me. When he comes forward I think there should be an award ceremony. Whoever he is, he should be up in front of the queen getting a medal for saving the life of Lexi Juby. He should be on the telly! Mother thinks it was some hippie traveller, and has left it at that. Owen is more interested. Last night he was going on about how we ought to go back and look for him, so I can thank him. But I don't want to go back in that place, and especially not with Owen. From what I can gather, it was once some sort of hospital, but no one seems to have much to say about it.

A massive fart rumbles up through the floorboards from the sitting room. That man is gross! Everything about Owen repels me. The way he looks, the way he smells. I hate his fat arse spilling out of too-tight jeans, and his nasty nylon work trousers and his revolting shiny black shoes. Imagine having him as a stepdad! Even his job makes me sick. He works as a security guard at the airport in immigration. He's there giving the evils to all the new arrivals, and sometimes he gets to go off on what he calls jollies. He told me about it

yesterday, when Mother was at work. He and three others go on aeroplanes to other countries, "escorting" failed asylum seekers home.

"Sometimes they scream," he said, grinning. "And sometimes they put up a fight; that's why we have to handcuff them."

"But they're not criminals," I said. "So why do you treat them so badly?"

"I'm not saying they're all bad people," said Owen. "I'm not prejudiced. But most of them come over here to scab off our welfare system, living off the taxes that I pay. They're just trying their luck. It's human nature."

"No, Owen," I said. "They come here to escape wars and stuff."

"You're naïve, Lexi," he said. "But then I like naïve girls."

"Oh sod off," I said, crossly. "You wouldn't talk to me like this if Mother was here. I wish someone would deport you."

I can't imagine how terrifying it must be, to be escorted home by Owen. He's always going on about how he had to thump someone to stop them breaking up the plane. Listen to me! Going on about politics. I suppose it's easy to pretend none of this stuff is happening when you're having a good time. But living here, with Owen telling his nasty stories, it's hard to avoid. I really don't know what Mother sees in him but I'm not really worried about her; she's the hardest person I know. She handles Owen just fine. No, it's me

58

I'm worried about. The whole time I've known Owen, it's like he's tracking me, circling me; waiting for the right moment to pounce.

I start on my make-up. As I'm looking pretty minging, I'm pulling out the big guns. I slap on foundation, bronzer, eye shadow, mascara, thick liquid eyeliner and lipgloss for the natural look.

When I'm done I let out a big sigh. At last I feel a bit more like me.

Downstairs, Mother is lying on her back on the kitchen floor with cucumber discs on her eyes, listening to her bridal relaxation CD. Currently she has only two topics of conversation: The Wedding (discussion of which makes her happy) or Tyson (which makes her sad and tearful). She's put posters up all over Bewlea about him, but no one has come forward. She and Owen have been to every dogs' home for miles around but have had no luck. It's like Tyson has just vanished into thin air. Because of this, Mother thinks he has been stolen.

"Maybe we should get Devlin to ask round all his contacts," I say, only half in jest.

Mother does not laugh. She's put a photograph of him in the kitchen window so I see him every time I wash up. I wish he'd come back. But at least the wedding helps to take her mind off him. There's so much to do. She wants to get married on her birthday next month, and although it's not going to be a big event, she's got to order the cake, get dresses, book a

photographer, sort out food, etc., etc. She's very busy with it all and hasn't got time to be sad about Tyson all the time.

The phone rings and I fly into the hallway to pick it up.

"Hello, Paula."

It's Dad! He thinks I am Mother.

"It's Lexi," I say, trying to keep my cool. "Where are you; why has your phone been switched off? Why haven't you called?"

"Lexi, are you all right?"

"No, I'm not." I tell him about the cellar and the dogs and finally how much I hate living here. "Can I come home?" I ask eventually. "Are you still in France?"

"Sorry, darling. There've been some complications." Then he goes on about me staying put for a while, because I needed looking after.

"I don't need looking after, I just want to go home!" I screech. "I've got to start college soon."

"Soon, babe, soon."

I ask him where he is and he says he can't say right now. I get annoyed then; it means he definitely is up to something dodgy.

"I hate you!" I scream and slam down the phone. I'm staring at the receiver, my eyes blurring with tears, when Owen pops his head into the hallway. "Has he finally come clean, then?"

"What? Come clean about what?" I stare at him. "What's going on?"

"That'll be a no, then," says Owen. But then Mother is here.

"Owen," she says warningly. She puts her hand on his arm, as if to lead him away.

"WHAT IS GOING ON WITH DAD?" I yell. "I'm not a kid, tell me."

Mother gives Owen the evils until he goes back to the telly. Then she takes a deep breath and squares up to me. "I can't tell you where your dad is right now, Lexi. I've made a promise. But he is OK. And he will come back. You will know more soon. I think you'll be staying with us at least another month. So I suggest we try and get on, shall we?"

Why can't she just tell me the truth? "No," I say. "Where's Dad?"

"Lexi. . ."

"Where's Dad, where's Dad, WHERE'S DAD?" I scream in her face. I know I'm being a head case but I can't stop myself and I don't care.

"You'll find out soon enough," says Mother, padding away in her pink cream satin slippers.

"BITCH," I scream at the back of her head. Mother hesitates, then keeps going. I pick up the phone and fling it to the floor just as Owen pounds back into the hallway.

"Don't speak to Paula like that. . ."

"Oh sod off." I push past him and run up to my room. I slam the door, which is clearly cliché action for a stressed teenager like myself, but it feels good. I open the door again and slam it again really hard and bits of wood fly on to the carpet. Time to put the brakes on, Lexi. Look at me! I'm acting like a female Devlin! I slump in the corner, looking at the picture of Manhattan.

It's scary how quickly you can end up on your own. A couple of weeks ago I had loads of people around me. Dad, Devlin, Chas and Moz were the important ones, but there was also all my mates from school. Here, I don't have anyone to talk to. I'm alone. No wonder I'm being such a bitch.

Missing

*I*n Bexton there were loads of places to go when I wanted to get out of the house. I could hang with the canal kids under the bridge, bench hop in the park, or I could just chill at Moz or Deb's house. Sometimes we'd just mess around on the school playing field, or walk into town and make one hot chocolate last for hours at Big Hilda's café. But here in Bewlea, I don't know where to go. I walk up and down the green, feeling self-conscious. If Moz wasn't in Cornwall I'd catch a bus and go and stay with her. Rain spots the duck pond. I stroke a lock of my hair and eye the dark clouds in the sky. I slouch up to the bus stop to check out the timetable when a poster catches my eye. At first I assume it is one of Mother's posters, but then I see the photo is of a different dog.

LOST PUPPY
Buttons
Male Jack Russell Terrier
Missing since 9th May
Reply 664367

Immediately beneath it is another poster. This one has been here for some time; the corners are curling in and the ink is all blurry. I can still read it, though.

MAYBELLE, Alsatian
LOST since 24th September
Small reward offered
Tel. 664345

It's August now, so Maybelle has been missing for nearly a year. Or maybe even longer judging by the state of the poster. I think of the dark figure I saw, running down our road, the dog bounding at his side, and wonder if there's a connection.

I've got about two pounds in my pocket so I decide to go into the post office store and buy some mints. A bell jingles as I open the door, and three faces look at me. One is a mean-faced bloke with a mullet and a gold earring, and a large German Shepherd dog at his heels. Then there's the woman behind the counter. She's short and thin with grey short hair and terrible maths-teacher-style glasses. There's also a powdery-faced old woman rummaging around with her walking stick in a basket of out-of-date crisps. Her bright-pink lipstick is slipping off over her cheek. Maybe she's been kissing some randy old granddad. Her fingers are choc-a-bloc with silver rings.

"Morning," I say and scoot into an aisle rammed full of tinned vegetables. It's a poky little shop and every surface is filled with cans and packets and jars of food. There's a vegetable rack, empty apart from some bendy-looking carrots and a whole stack of dusty postcards, most of them in lurid seventies-style colours, of Bewlea village green and surrounding buildings. But as I flip through them I find a black and white shot of a group of people in old-fashioned clothes standing on the steps of a large, imposing building with a clock tower. I flip it over and read that it is the house-keeping staff of Beacon Hospital, taken in the 1920s. Only in the photo the windows have glass in them and there are no weeds growing up over the steps. It's weird seeing the house looking all together, and imagining those people working inside. At the bottom of the pile is a postcard picturing a statue of a woman. It looks familiar.

"Lady Fallondale." The pink-lipstick woman is at my elbow. She's got a bit of a moustache. "Wife of the founder of Beacon Hospital. The rumour has it he did her in and buried her under the padded cells."

I nod, remembering the statue outside Beacon Hospital. I smile at the old woman and shuffle round to the shop notice board. I read advertisements for sacks of potatoes, aquariums and grass-cutting services. I look closer. Another missing puppy!

LOST, MOLLY
Collie puppy
Nervous disposition
5 months old

There's something seriously weird going on.

"Some say there's a dog thief who comes up from Plymouth." Pink-lips-walking-stick-woman reappears at my side.

"All these lost dogs," I say. "Haven't any of them ever been found?"

"Of course," says the woman. She lowers her voice. "That man buying cheese." She points to mullet-man. "His puppy went missing but came home after a week. No one knew where he'd been. I think he'd just wandered off and got lost." She looks at me. "You're a pretty girl. You're not from round here, are you?"

"I'm visiting my mother," I say, smiling at her. It's nice to be called pretty, even by a mad old woman. I point to a new card stuck on the corner of the notice board.

LOST DOG
Dobermann cross
8 months old
Reward offered
Tel. 664889

"That's her dog."

"I'm so sorry," says the woman. She leans in close and I get a waft of her sweet stale breath. "Where did you say your mother lives?"

"I didn't, but it's Houndswood Estate," I say.

"We call it The Bronx at my end of the village," says the woman, looking at me harder. "Everyone says all those new houses ruined the character of the village, but I like a bit of life." She grabs my hand and her stick clatters to the floor. "Ooh," she says, "are you the girl who nearly drowned up at the Beacon?" I nod. Fame at last. "I'm Emily Prior," she says. "I'd love to hear about what happened to you."

"Mrs Prior, you're such an old gossip." Mullet-man is just behind us. He gives me a grin. "Lucas Neasdon." He holds out his hand. "And this is Toad." He points to his dog.

"Hello, Lucas," I say, keeping my hands firmly by my sides. I turn to Emily. "I'll tell you all about it, only I'm in a bit of a rush."

"Come and see me," says Emily. "I'm at number four. Hope Street." She looks at me anxiously. "You don't mind me asking, do you, dear? Only when you get old, it can get a bit lonely."

"Mrs Prior, you're about as lonely as cloud in a thunderstorm," says Lucas Neasdon.

"Of course I don't mind," I say, ignoring him. "I'll come and see you in the next few days."

I leave the shop, sucking on a mint. Emily Prior might not be what I had in mind when I hoped I'd make some new mates, but I've got a bit of a soft spot where old ladies are concerned. I don't know why. Maybe I feel sorry for them, with their stiff knees, wrinkly faces and bad handbags.

The bell above the shop door jingles as it swings open.

"Nice to meet you too, Lexi Juby." Lucas Neasdon brushes past.

How does he know my name? I don't remember telling it to Emily. Maybe I did and I've forgotten. I walk on but watch out of the corner of my eye as Neasdon and his dog jump into a white van and roar off. Something tells me I haven't seen the last of them.

Emily

"So what did he look like exactly?"

"I don't know – exactly." I'm trying to eat my breakfast (one slice of toast, a banana and a mug of black, sweet coffee) but Owen keeps bugging me with all these questions about the bloke who rescued me.

"You must have some idea," he persists, shovelling fried eggs into his mouth. I try to think, just to humour him.

"He had dark, curly hair," I say. "A bit of a beard. He was scruffy-looking."

"You've said all that before," says Owen, wiping yellow yolk from his mouth with the back of his hand. "Give me details: was he fat? Thin? What colour were his eyes? What was he wearing?"

"I was pretty out of it," I say. "And it was dark. But I think he was quite skinny." I take a bite of toast and watch as Mother bustles around the kitchen, scrubbing surfaces and slamming frying pans into the dishwasher. She and Owen had a row last night. I heard raised voices through my bedroom wall. They were trying to keep it quiet so I don't know what it was about, but there is definitely tension in the air this morning.

"What did he say? Did you notice an accent?"

"I can't remember what he said," I reply, beginning to feel annoyed. It's not nice to be interrogated before you've even finished your breakfast. "I was half drowned, I was scared; I wasn't recording everything he said."

"You must remember something," says Owen, exasperated.

I do remember the stranger was quite nice-looking, in a rough kind of way. But I don't tell Owen this.

"Why don't you leave her alone?" says Mother suddenly. "I don't know why you're so bothered anyway. You asked her all this before."

Owen grunts. "Just taking an interest," he says. "You know, there's been some funny types hanging around up at the hospital since it closed down. There might even be a connection with your dog, Paula."

"Don't," says Mother. "Don't go there." She's still cut up about Tyson. She's had a photograph of him blown up and laminated, with MISSING, ENQUIRE WITHIN printed on the bottom, and has attached it to the front gate. She's still putting fresh water in Tyson's bowl every day, just in case he strolls in through the door.

"I'm only trying to help." Owen drops his fork and pushes his breakfast away. He goes into the hallway and I hear him take his shoes from the rack. In less than a minute he's out the door.

I look at Mother. "What's bugging him?" I ask.

"Me, probably," says Mother.

I'm shocked. She doesn't usually confide in me like

that. But then a hard look comes over her face. "You need something to do," she says. "You've been moping around the house too long and Owen likes to have a bit of quiet sometimes."

She picks up Owen's plate, scrapes it and puts it in the dishwasher. "We need help in the kitchens at the hotel. It's not riches and the work isn't glamorous." She looks me up and down. "But you won't mind that."

"But I'm going home soon," I cut in.

"We'll see. Lexi, you need to get out of the house. I know you've had a nasty experience but you need to move on."

A *nasty* experience? Nearly drowning in a dark pit of filthy water . . . *nasty*? I can't bring myself to look at her.

"The pay isn't much," Mother says, unwrapping a dishwasher tablet. "But you'd like the money, I expect."

"What you've given me hasn't gone very far," I spit. She's only given me five pounds since I've been here. Luckily Dad gave me fifty quid to tide me over. Naturally I haven't told Mother about this.

Mother eyes my half eaten toast. She wants to wash up my plate. I feel like I can't do anything in this house, even finish my breakfast. "They can offer you twenty hours a week." I feel like telling her where to stick her kitchen skivvy job. The reason I'm going to do my A-levels is so that I don't have to do grimy jobs. But I do need the money and I'm going insane with boredom.

"All right," I say, before I change my mind. "But if it's pants I'm not sticking it."

"Good," says Mother. "You can start tonight."

"I'll need some new clothes," I say, never one to miss an opportunity.

"No, what you've got is fine," says Mother. "When you get your first pay packet, I'll drive you to the shops."

I don't start in the kitchens until six o'clock tonight so I have an entire day to kill. Mother and Owen are out so at least I've got the place to myself. I've done forty-five minutes of exercises (focusing on the bum area) and experimented with a new "up" hairdo. I've showered, shaved my legs, washed and blow-dried my hair. (Oh, for some hair straighteners.) I've moisturized my entire body and put on my make-up. I've ironed my clothes for the week and given myself a mini-manicure. I've cleaned and vacuumed my bedroom. What now? If I was at home in Bexton I'd probably go out and get the ingredients for tonight's dinner, but Mother doesn't like my cooking, and besides, neither of us is going to be here to eat it, and no way am I cooking for that fat ape Mother is marrying. I go downstairs and tidy up a bit. In the kitchen, I look at Tyson's bed, the covers all hairy and grubby, and wonder if I should give it a wash. I decide against it. Mother might take it the wrong way and think I'm trying to erase all traces of him, or something like that.

I switch on the TV. The first thing that comes on is the local news reporting about that woman who was at the hospital the same time as me, Nyasha Agruba. The reporter is standing next to a massive fence, and beyond it is a tall grey building. It's a detention centre. He goes on about how Nyasha and her son will be brought here before she is deported. Then the film cuts back to a village hall where loads of people are shouting. Then he interviews some of the people outside. It's Charlton, the next village along from Bewlea.

"She should be sent home," says one old witch. "This country is too crowded as it is."

"Let her stay," says another old dear. "She's a lovely woman. What difference will it make?" Oh wow, that was Emily! She's still wearing that awful pink lipstick.

I watch the rest of the report, then switch off the TV. It's too depressing to spend a whole morning watching television. It makes me feel dead. Besides, I really will get fat if I sit around on my bum all day. I wish I had just one friend in this bloody village. Someone to call on. Somewhere to go. Then I have an idea and I run up the stairs to Mother's room. I rummage through her make-up until I find what I'm looking for.

Outside there's a faint taste of ice in the air. It's late August but it feels like winter is already on the way. I shiver. Some summer this has been.

Number four Hope Street is pink with a black door and black sills. It has gnomes in the garden. The sight of these gnomes makes me stop in my tracks. It's time for a change of plan. I decide to go home and cut out my split ends. But as I am heading up the hill, I hear a familiar voice.

"Lex-ie, are you lost?" So there's nothing for me to do but stop, slowly turn and give a weak grin. Emily waves from the doorstep. "Come in, don't be shy," she sings, ushering me up the steps into her house. It smells stale. She needs to open the windows and get some carpet powder. Nasty floral wallpaper with hideously mismatched flower prints line the walls. There are matching vases of plastic flowers on the mantelpiece and the thick pink carpet needs a vacuum. I look around, waiting for someone, I don't know who, to put in an appearance. It just feels like someone else probably lives here.

"It's just me," says Emily, watching me. "Tea?"

I knew there would be cups and saucers, and I wasn't surprised they were just a little bit grubby, like Emily hadn't washed them in hot water. There were a couple of photographs, but they looked dead old. I decide the serious-faced young couple were Emily's grandparents. No kiddy photos line the walls. No grandchildren, then. My nan's house is rammed full of kiddy photos because no one knows what else to give her for Christmas. No one wants to give her anything decent because she'll probably die fairly soon and it would be a waste. I decline a stale-looking digestive and sit on the edge of a flowered armchair.

"So nice to have a visitor," says Emily, settling her bulk in a chair opposite mine and looking at me expectantly. "Since I did this," she taps her leg, "I'm not out and about as much as I'd like." I can't stop looking at her moustache. I hope she doesn't realize.

"I've got something for you," I say, holding out a lipstick. "It's *Ruby Kiss*. That pink shade is nice in spring, but it doesn't do justice to your skin tone. You'd suit a darker tone. Here." I pass it over.

Emily rolls the lipstick in her palm. "Thank you," she says, looking surprised. "But it's an expensive one."

"It's an investment," I say. "Cheap make-up only makes you look cheap. Here. Let me put some on for you." I don't expect she has a lippy brush so I do my best, smearing the colour on her mouth and trying to ignore the soft bristles of her moustache brushing against my wrist. When I'm done, Emily goes to look at herself in the mirror.

"That's lovely, dear," she says.

"You really need sealer, and maybe some eyeshadow so you're not bottom-heavy, but the colour suits you." I smile at her, wondering if I should bring round some *Immac* hair-removal cream next time.

"I feel eighteen again," sighs Emily.

If I come here again, I could bring some of Mother's blusher. Mother has lots of make-up suitable for older skin.

"Everyone in the village is talking about you," says Emily. "About your escape."

I nod. "What is that place? Why is it empty?"

"You don't know?" asks Emily. I say nothing. I'm not

the sort of person who asks a question if I already know the answer.

"It was built in the middle of the nineteenth century." She looks at me closely. "That's the eighteen-hundreds."

"Yes," I say. She thinks I'm stupid. Never mind; it's sometimes easier if people think you're thick. It's like wearing a disguise.

"It was built as a lunatic asylum," says Emily. "It started off quite upmarket, you know. As well as the genuine lunatics, ladies got sent there when their husbands got sick of them. Depressed gentle folks went there too. Or high-born daughters who had been led astray, if you catch my meaning."

I smile sweetly at her. I wish someone would try and lead me astray.

"As the years passed, it changed hands several times and went downhill," Emily continues. "There were some high-profile scandals. An inspector discovered that a woman had been chained up in the same room for ten years, and once a madman escaped and ran naked through Bewlea High Street. It became more and more notorious, until even the most wicked husband couldn't send his wife there and get away with it in polite society."

"Are you married, Emily?" I butt in, sensing some history here.

"I was married for one month," she replies. "One week in bliss, one week in horror and two weeks camping on the solicitor's doorstep."

"Can you get divorced in two weeks?" I ask. This might be handy information if, as I suspect, Mother gets tired of Owen sooner rather than later.

"Marriage isn't everything," sighs Emily, not answering.

I've always assumed I'd get married eventually. Not until I'm quite old, though; maybe twenty-four or twenty-five. I'd quite like to marry Prince William, though he is a bit old for me. I quite fancy being Princess Lexi. I'd employ my dad and my brother to keep away the paparazzi. Sadly I don't think I'll marry him because I'll never be able to afford to go skiing, so I'm unlikely ever to meet him. There is also the question of me being rather common, but he would see through my humble ways to my wit and of course my devastating beauty. I don't expect he'd want to consort with my brother, though. I suppose I could have a shot at Prince Harry, Devlin could take him out clubbing, but he seems a bit of a wild card, and I'm fed up with them.

"You're miles away," says Emily, and I give myself a little shake and attempt to focus on what she is telling me.

Beacon House Asylum took in the mentally ill until the turn of the last century; then in the early 1900s it had a revamp and became known as Beacon House Hospital. During the Second World War, the army requisitioned three of the wings and it got trashed. After the war it opened again for another twenty years; then the government closed it down and it was left empty for years. Eventually the council bought it up and put a new roof on it, the high fence was put up and the north and east wings were converted into a detention centre for illegal immigrants – people the government were planning to deport. The rest of Beacon House Hospital was left to rot.

"The detention centre closed down five years ago," says Emily. "I hope it's for good this time. It was always a sad, dark place; depressing to work in and miserable for those incarcerated there."

"I'm not too fond of it myself," I mutter.

"I think they should burn the whole place down," she says. "If you had drowned, you wouldn't have been the first to come to a sticky end up there."

I lean forward. "What do you mean?"

Emily hesitates. She swallows a mouthful of tea, and then she lets out a long sigh. "A year after it closed, some intruders found a woman's body up there, in a shallow grave."

I shiver. "Who was she?"

"Nobody knows," says Emily. "They couldn't identify her."

"You know a lot about it," I say.

"I ought to," says Emily, taking another sip of tea and leaving a faint brown stain on her upper lip. "I worked there on and off for fifty years."

"I started in the fifties, after the war," Emily tells me. "I was an upper-maid and I was eventually promoted to housekeeper; this was when it was Beacon House Hospital. Then it closed down and everyone lost their jobs. The place was empty for years. Everyone thought it was going to be demolished, but then, out of the blue, they turned part of it into a detention centre. I got myself a little job in the kitchens. It was strange working there again after all those years." She looks at me. "Half the village used to be employed up there. It devastated the village when it was closed down yet again. It was like history repeating itself. Your mother's boyfriend must have told you about it."

"No," I say. "Why would he?"

"He worked up there when it was a detention centre," says Emily. "He was on security."

He never told me that! He said nothing at all about it. Why, the sneaky so and so.

"Most people round here would like to see Beacon Hospital razed to the ground," says Emily. "It's not a happy place. More tea?" I shake my head. My mouth still feels tainted from the last cup. I look at my watch and am surprised to see I've been here half an hour already.

"Is there a caretaker working up there?" I ask. "I don't know who saved me."

"It's looked after by a security firm," says Emily. "They come and go. I have no idea who rescued you. You were lucky. Don't go there again, will you? You might not be so lucky next time."

A bang somewhere out the back makes us jump,

and Emily slops tea into her lap. "That'll be the stray," says Emily. "You stay here; he's very shy." She creaks out of her chair and shuffles off to investigate. I look around the room. I wonder what I'll be like when I'm old. Will I, like Emily, surround myself with flower pictures and photographs of dead relatives? There's a newspaper on the chair, and, as Emily doesn't seem to be coming back and I've got nothing else to do, I pick it up and skim the front page.

I hear more scuffling and creaking, like a stiff window is being lowered.

AGRUBA FAMILY TO BE DEPORTED

Failed asylum seeker Nyasha Agruba and her son Chuma, 11, are to be deported by the Home Office early next month.

Nyasha arrived in the UK six years ago from Zimbabwe after her journalist husband, Farai Agruba, was detained on charges of conspiracy. He is still imprisoned. Nyasha has settled in the village of Charlton and residents have come out in force to oppose her deportation. "It amounts to a death sentence," says Delia Freely, a teacher at the local primary school, which Chuma Agruba has attended for the last five years. "After Nyasha's husband was detained, Nyasha lived in fear for her safety. We can't allow her to be sent back." A Home Office spokeswoman says, "There are many of these cases. Everyone gets a fair trial. We cannot allow everyone to stay."

I hear more scuffling and creaking, like a stiff window is being lowered.

"Emily," I call, "are you OK?"

"Yes, yes," calls Emily. "I'll be back in a minute. Please don't worry."

"Do you need help?"

"No," calls Emily firmly. "I don't want to scare it." I sit back and watch the minutes tick by on Emily's big grandfather clock. She's taking ages. I get up and have a poke round the room. The skirting boards are thick with dust and the grimy doors could do with a wipe with a hot cloth. The windows are covered in smears. Maybe Emily's so old she finds it hard to do the housework. Would it be rude to offer to help out a bit? I open a door leading off the dining room. It's a tiny, dark room. It smells musty and cobwebs hang from the walls. I see a mountain of tins of food piled up to the ceiling. There's sweetcorn and tinned mushrooms and cans of tomatoes, potatoes, peas, kidney beans, butter beans and about forty cans of baked beans. She's got canned meats and sausages. Boxes of dried dog food are stacked neatly in the window. Some people like storing up stuff. There's a man on our street at home in Bexton who collects rainwater in bottles and buckets. He keeps it in a big tank in his garden. He says it's in case the terrorists poison the water supply. Maybe Emily is like him.

"Lexi?" I feel a hand on my shoulder. I didn't hear her coming.

"Oh, sorry, I was looking for the loo."

Emily sees me glancing back at the baked bean mountain.

"I like to feel prepared," she says. "I was snowed in for three weeks in 1976, and I lived off flour pastry and raisins. You can't be too careful these days."

I tell Emily that I'm going home.

"Do come again, dear," she says. She looks worried. "But only if you want to. I know you young people have lots to do."

My head is buzzing as I walk home. I'm glad I didn't know Beacon House Hospital was a lunatic asylum when I was stuck up there. It would have freaked me out. I could still be down in that forgotten cellar, dead and drowned and grotesque. But I'm not. I was rescued. But by whom?

Later, when I mention to Mother that I've visited Emily, she looks at me in surprise.

"That old lady with the stick?"

I nod.

"She pops up everywhere," says Mother. "There's nothing that happens in this village that she doesn't know about. I think other people's lives are her hobby. It's sad really. You'd better be careful what you tell her, Lexi, because half the village will know the next day."

"I quite liked her," I say.

Mother looks at me thoughtfully. "I wonder if she can do calligraphy. Old people often have nice handwriting."

"And why is that?" I ask.

"I need someone to do the placement cards," says Mother. I look at her blankly. "You know, for the wedding meal. Ooh, and she could do the order of ceremony." Mother is half talking to herself. "Is it worth inviting her so I can ask her to write them out for me?"

"Mother," I say wearily. "Get a life."

Ella

Three weeks later, no word from Dad and I'm still here, in Houndswood Estate, living with Mother and the Australopithecine. Wedding madness has descended on the household. The place is full of leaflets advertising bridal music, coach and horses, his 'n' hers jewellery and bargain-basement cosmetic surgery. Mother is on a bridal diet, which means she hardly eats anything. I feel like a right pig when I trough down over lunch and she's worrying about the calorific content of her lettuce. She's off to Bexton next week for a wedding-dress consultation. She's going with Celia, her geriatric bridesmaid. I would have refused to go with her, but it would have been nice to be asked. It's the sort of thing I imagine normal mothers and daughters would do (though possibly it would be the daughter choosing her wedding dress, not the mother choosing hers). I've spent a lot of time thinking about the wedding; from what I can see, Mother and Owen don't actually get on that well together. One minute they're all over each other, the next they're at each other's throats. I think Mother is marrying him because she's desperate and doesn't think she can do better. But she can. She's not bad-looking for someone of her age.

I hope I never get that desperate.

I'm working five shifts a week in the hotel, doing waitressing, washing up, and helping the chef. I'm quite at home there now I know everyone. There's the head chef, Wendy, who can get a bit stressy, but nothing I can't handle. More importantly, there're people my age; Ella does waitressing. She's cool. She takes the piss out of everyone, but in a nice way. She's easy to talk to. She's tall and blonde with amazing grey eyes. Like me, she hasn't got a boyfriend at the moment either. There's also Jak, who only arrived last month and lives in the hotel. He's here just for the summer. He does most of the washing up and must be about eighteen. Ella says he's from Eastern Europe somewhere. He's quite shy, has a bum-fluff beard, thick glasses and his English isn't so hot. He's got a nice face but he's not my type. He's too stocky for me, and also I like outgoing men. But it's nice to be around people who aren't geriatrics, and it's fantastic to be earning money again. Sometimes Mother is working at the same time as me but I only get glimpses of her because she rarely comes into the kitchens. Everyone hates the boss, Mr Middleton. He's a slime-bucket with curly, grey hair. He wears checked suits with flowered cravats and a silk hanky popping out of his pocket. He thinks he is very important and devastatingly attractive. He'll come into the kitchens when we're mad busy and ask me to knock him up a sandwich, right now! And give me a wink, as if it is my secret desire to make him food. I don't mind doing donkey-work, but I don't like being treated like a donkey. But work is all right. And it's lovely having some money, and I've saved up enough to buy new straighteners.

The lunch shift is over. Me, Ella and Jak are sitting by the bins outside the kitchens, eating leftovers, and I'm telling them about the dogs attacking me. Ella says for years people have been talking about a wild dog roaming the woods. It's like a local legend. I say it's not a legend, there's more than one, and we need to get the SAS out to finish them off. We get talking about the bloke who rescued me. I tell them how I woke up in only my underwear, wrapped in a quilt. I find this heavy stuff but Ella thinks it's hilarious.

"So, are you sure he didn't . . . you know. . ."

I know exactly what she means but I wait for her to spell it out. Jak is even quieter than usual. I think he's embarrassed.

"Do you think he interfered with you?" goes on Ella.

Jak coughs a little and rustles the pages of his comic book. He says he reads them to improve his English.

"No," I say. This is something I'm sure about. Whoever he was, he rescued me from that cellar, hauled me up on the rope and left me somewhere safe. He even left me food.

"I'd like to know who he is," I say, chewing on a bread roll. "Everyone says he was probably a tramp, passing through." Jak looks up from his plate of cold chips. I never really know how much he understands. I think he might fancy either Ella or me, or both of us. It doesn't matter. He's harmless. He can be quite funny sometimes, and he must get bored. Living in the hotel all the time would drive me nuts.

"Maybe we could go and find him," says Jak suddenly. "I like trees."

Ella catches my eye and grins. "Yeah, right," she says. "You just want a romantic walk with our newest member of staff here."

"No, no," blushes Jak. "I mean, yes . . . but. . ."

"Leave him alone," I tell Ella, giving her a nudge. She's trouble, but I like her a lot. I've only known her a short while but she's already a friend. I've not told her much, only that I'm temporarily living with my mother. She's asked me a few questions but she's sussed out I don't want to say much, and hasn't taken it any further. She's big, much heavier than me, but she's not fat. She's just tall, with long arms and legs, and she's well-covered. I feel thin and small next to her, which is nice, but at the same time, I like the way her arms look. The skin is all golden and kind of plump, but not in a bad way. They're peachy. Mine are brown and thin, maybe even a bit scrawny. It's interesting. She's much bigger than me, but she looks good. I never thought I'd think that. She's just about to go to university and is working at the hotel to earn some money. She has high hopes of scoring a boyfriend or three when she gets to university. I say she could pass them on to me when she's sick of them. She's quite posh but she isn't stuck-up.

She's a find!

Top Table

The village is under siege. There have been loads of burglaries. At work everyone's talking about it. The post office store was broken into last night. Apparently the CCTV showed a hooded figure shoving food into a sack.

"This happens sometimes," Ella says over a stack of greasy meat pans. She leans over and removes a cloud of foam from my nose. "Every now and then there's a crime spree; then it all goes quiet for ages. Some people reckon it's to do with the travellers passing through. But some of us think there's a resident Bewlea Burglar."

The kitchen door swings open and Mr Middleton, the boss, struts in. He's wearing a yellow cravat. He looks ridiculous. Oh no, he's heading our way. I pretend to be deeply absorbed in my washing-up.

"Are you eighteen?" he asks Ella. She nods. "Then come and help out behind the bar. I wish you girls would use your initiative. It's crazy out there." He looks at me. "And you can go out and collect and wash some glasses."

We dry our hands and check our reflections in the huge, shiny metal saucepans. I could do with a slick of lipgloss but I left my make-up bag at home. I'll have to face the punters as I am. The bar is rammed. I'm edging round the tables, collecting empties, when I feel a hand on the small of my back.

"Hello, babe," says Owen. I hadn't known he was in tonight. He's sitting with three other men. One of them is the man from the post office. I can't remember his name. But I remember his dog, Toad, who is staring at me from under the table. "It's time you met the blood brothers," says Owen. I move away from his hand, taken aback at how similar the three men look. They all have thick hair growing low down on their brows. They have to be related.

"This is my right-hand man, Lucas," says Owen. "Lucas, this is my new stepdaughter." Eek.

"Hello again, darling," says Lucas. He's wearing a pink, very ironed shirt and lots of aftershave. He turns to Owen. "Is she sixteen?"

"Ask my mother," I say. "You'll find her at reception." They all laugh. I don't.

"I'm Matty; I'm his left-hand man," says a stocky man with very short gelled-up hair. "I bet you've never met triplets before."

"Nope," I say, pretending to be unimpressed, though really I want to whip out my phone and take a picture to send to Moz.

You'll never guess what I've just seen.

"Anyway, I've got work to do. . ."

"And this is Johnny. . ." says Owen. "Don't be put off

by his size; he couldn't fight his way out of a paper bag." Even sitting down, Johnny towers over the others. He's wearing a red tartan lumberjack shirt and he needs a shave. I glance coldly at him and he goes red and looks away.

"She hates me," says Owen, grinning all over his stupid handsome face. "Don't you, Lexi?"

"Do I?" I say, turning to go. But Owen has grabbed my wrist.

"She's cute, isn't she?" he says, breathing beer breath at me. I feel my face getting hot as all four of them stare. "I'm going away for three days," he says. "You gonna miss me?"

"No," I say, looking down at his meaty fingers. "Let go, please."

"A big job, this one," says Owen, holding on tightly. "I might get on the telly. I'm escorting Nyasha Agruba back to her homeland."

"Everyone says she's gonna put up a fight," says Matty. "You'd better watch yourself, mate."

"Owen," interrupts Johnny. "Let Lexi go. She's got work to do."

"Oops, sorry Lexi, I was practising my restraints," says Owen, winking at the others.

I slip my arm out of Owen's sweaty grasp and turn to him. "I don't know how you can live with yourself."

Owen laughs. "I didn't make up the rules, darling. I just do as I'm told. I'm just earning the money which puts a roof over your head." I think of the TV footage I've seen of Nyasha Agruba. She looked small and vulnerable.

"Treat her properly," I say.

"I'll wear my kid gloves," says Owen, and they all laugh, except Johnny, who looks faintly embarrassed.

"These things are never as bad as the news makes out," he says to me in his soft, gruff voice. "They blow things up to make a story."

"Perhaps you should try telling that to Nyasha Agruba," I say and walk off, hearing sniggering behind my back. I flee through the swinging doors into the kitchens and press my burning face against the cool metal of the refrigerator. What's the matter with me? I'm not normally fazed by lairy blokes. I must be going soft.

Ella bursts in. "You all right, babe?" I tell her what happened.

"Gross," she says. "The Neasdon triplets are trouble, except Johnny. He's cool; he's so big he doesn't need to throw his weight around. Stay away from the other two, though, especially Lucas, the mullet-man. Want me to gob in their drinks when I get them the next round?" I decline, slightly shocked. "Okey-dokes." She grins and has a slug of Coke.

"It's Owen," I say. "I can't stand the thought of him being my stepfather. It makes me feel sick."

"Can't say I'd fancy it myself." Ella chews ice thoughtfully. "You have to talk to your mum, then," she says. She waggles her finger at me. "But don't go overboard. Remember, love is blind."

I watch her back as she swishes through the saloon

doors into the bar. Love is blind? I think Mother must have lost all her senses where Owen's concerned.

I have the next evening off, and I'm watching the local TV news in the front room waiting to see if Nyasha Agruba gets a mention. But just before the news, Mother comes in with her pink wedding folder. She's looking dead thin. All the dieting is paying off.

"I need your help," she says. She sounds dreamy and not quite here, like she's not had enough sleep.

"Sure," I mumble as the headlines come up. Sure enough, there's a shot of Nyasha and her son being bundled into a white van by a tough-looking woman. And lurking behind them is Owen himself, looking smug and official in his security officer uniform.

"Look!" I tell Mother, pointing at the screen.

We watch in silence. We only see Owen for a few seconds before the next news item comes on.

Mother sighs. "He looks handsome in his uniform, doesn't he?" She sounds sad. "I suppose it would be tacky for him to wear it at the wedding."

I grimace. "Very tacky."

"And looks aren't everything, are they?" she says, half to herself. I can hardly believe what I'm hearing. *Looks aren't everything?* Mother is obsessed with appearances. She's always nagging about a loose thread here or a smear there, or what she considers a mismatched outfit. And me – it may be shallow, but I can't imagine not wanting to look good.

Mother sighs again and gives herself a little shake. "I don't know what to do about the top table," she says, turning away from the TV. "You know, for the wedding meal."

I stare at her. There are matters of life and death going on here, and at the very least, her fiancé has just made his TV debut. And she's worried about where people are going to sit for dinner. I switch off the television.

"I don't know how to fit everyone in; there's only room for six, and there's me and Owen, and Auntie Flo and Uncle Paul, and Devlin and you of course, and Owen says he wants his mum. But that's seven. That's too many." She looks at me. I can see snakes winding behind her eyes. I can feel myself losing it. Don't do it, Lexi. Don't do it. Don't fly off the handle like a little kid.

"Just come out and say it, why don't you?" I say. "You want me off the top table. I'm only your daughter; I'm not even your bridesmaid." I'm getting worked up now. I can't stop myself. "I don't know why you bother asking me about this at all. You've worked it all out already."

"No I haven't," says Mother. "I. . ." But I don't let her speak. I start screaming about how she's never liked me and how I'm not. . .

"I do like you," interrupts Mother. "Mostly." That shuts me right up. "Though you're quite hard work at the moment," she says. There's a long pause in which I gather myself together. I have to tell her. It's now or never.

"We have to talk about Owen," I say, building up to deliver my diplomatic, well-thought-out spiel. All at once it feels like the room is shrinking around us, and Mother has lost that dreamy look in her eyes and is right here staring at me.

He makes me feel uneasy.

I'm not ready to think of him as my stepdad.

I'm not sure he's going to make you happy.

He says inappropriate things to me.

But Mother strikes first. "You don't like him and you don't want me to marry him," she says. "Correct?"

"Yes," I say, forgetting what I was going to say next.

"He finds you difficult too," says Mother. "Though at least he makes an effort. Unlike you."

"But he's a perv," I screech, forgetting my rehearsed speech. "He's always saying dodgy stuff."

"Like what?" asks Mother, not taking her eyes off me. But I can't think of a single thing. I can't believe it. My mind has gone blank.

"He didn't let go of my wrist last night in the pub," I say eventually. "He said I was cute. I was scared."

Mother snorts. "I can't believe you're scared of anything, Lexi."

"And he's vile about that poor woman they're deporting."

"It's his job," says Mother. "He's a professional. He can't afford to get attached."

"But he's so gross. . ."

"That's enough," barks Mother. "You wonder why I

95

haven't asked you to be bridesmaid? To sit at the top table? To help me with my dress? It's because you make it hard for me to include you. You're so rude to Owen I'm ashamed. You aren't happy for us at all. Why should you be part of the celebrations?"

For once I have absolutely nothing to say. The thing is, she's right. I'm not happy for her. I don't want them to get married because I think Owen is horrible and he's driving Mother and me even further apart.

"But I don't think you're sure," I say, not knowing where these words are coming from. "You're so wrapped up in all the organizing, you're not thinking about what you're actually doing."

Mother picks up her mobile and starts fiddling with it. "You're sixteen, Lexi Juby. You know nothing about love."

I suddenly get a waft of Owen's aftershave. I don't know where it's coming from. It makes me want to gag. I have to get outside. I elbow past Mother and rush outside, slamming the door. I stand on the steps, inhaling the night air. I hear a distant roar and look up to see the orange lights of an aeroplane flash through the night sky. Maybe that's Nyasha's plane. I watch it till it's gone. Then everything is quiet except for the hum and crackle of the electricity pylon.

I'm lying in bed, turning over and back again. I can't sleep. My arms get in the way and my neck aches whichever way I lie. I can hear the hall clock, ticking away. It's just chimed two a.m. I'm having the same thoughts over and over again, like when's Dad going to take me home out of all this? I'm supposed to be starting college in September, and at this rate, it's not going to happen. Where is he? I'm going to look really rough if I don't get some sleep soon. On impulse I climb out of bed and pull open the curtains. The moonlight streams in. I stand by the window and look out at the back garden and beyond to the rows of houses and the orange street lights. I'd rather be anywhere but here. It's Friday night; I should be at a party, or a club, dancing with my mates. I should be out in the world, not stuck in this boring house in this boring place. I open the window and stick my head out and take some deep breaths. I stare for so long that my eyes start playing tricks on me and I see faces mould themselves out of the cracks in the buildings and the shadows on the street.

But then I hear it and a chill shoots over my skin.

The howling.

I'm woken by a noise downstairs. It's a bump, the sound of something heavy falling on a carpet. I'm wide awake. I grab for my mobile and read the time. 03.07. My room is still bright with moonlight. Everything looks like it has been outlined with a silver pen: my chair, the window with the curtains I have forgotten to close, and my tiny TV are all glowing. I know that it's the Bewlea Burglar. I can almost hear his feet on Mother's cream carpet, looking at her books, her glassware, the plasma screen TV and the DVD player. Then I hear a rattle in the kitchen. I find myself creeping out of my room and across the landing. I've got my mobile gripped in my hand, ready to dial 999. I listen at Mother's door and hear her softly breathing, long, slow breaths that tell me she is in a deep sleep, blinded by her mask and made deaf by her earplugs. What's the best thing to do? I'm not exactly scared, more curious. This is probably some dopey teenager like Devlin rifling though our stuff. I may even know him! If I call the police now, they'll be here in maybe twenty minutes. He might have gone by then. I wonder what Devlin would do if he'd got caught red-handed like this. I suppose having a brother like Devlin means I'm not too alarmed by this situation.

Then I remember I left my new straighteners down there. Without stopping to think, I'm charging down the stairs.

"Bugger off!" I shout, bursting into the kitchen. I fumble for the light switch and blink in the sudden brilliance. I blink again.

It's him.

Sausages

A lad of about eighteen stares at me with big dark eyes. He's got tan-coloured skin, a ratty beard and a mop of black, curling, matted hair. He's wearing raggedy grey trousers and a dirty red bomber jacket that's too small for him. He's taller than me but he's pretty skinny. His toes stick out the ends of his wellies. He's dirty and he also stinks.

"Hello again," I say. He looks at me and I remember I am only wearing my short nightie. I cross my arms over my chest. "You saved my life, remember? Thanks for that." He appears to be transfixed. I step behind the cooker to hide my legs. In one hand he's holding a sack and in the other, a can of frankfurters.

"I wouldn't bother with those," I say, pointing to the sausages. "They taste like old pants." He says nothing, but a grin slowly spreads across his face. "You'd be better off with the ones in the fridge; they're fresh from the butcher," I say. He smiles at me some more and despite everything, I find myself smiling back.

"So what's all this about, then?" I ask. I'm absolutely not afraid. For one thing, this man has saved my life so is unlikely to do me over now. Also, Mother is only one

99

scream away. Also, I can tell, ninety-eight per cent, that he fancies me. His pupils are enormous and he can't take his eyes off me. Oh God! I remember that he has seen me nearly naked. He's washed me off and wrapped me up in an eiderdown, and carried me to a safe place. I look away from his bright eyes. "So what'd you do with Tyson, then?" I ask. "Only my mother would quite like him back."

"Uh?" he says in a gruff, grunty voice and raises his eyebrows, the grin never faltering.

"Dog?" I say. "It was you who nicked him, wasn't it?"

The lad looks at the door and then at me. He's not smiling any more; he looks scared.

"What is it?" I ask. I hear the front door slam into the wall as it is flung open. Feet pound over the hall towards us. I haven't got time to think but I don't like this. The kitchen door flies open and Owen barges into the room.

"I knew it!" he roars. "I saw you through the window." He grabs for the intruder but the boy jumps right over the breakfast bar to the other side of the room.

"Shouldn't you be in a plane?" I ask conversationally.

"Grab him!" bellows Owen. As if. The boy is leaping round like a monkey; I wouldn't catch him in a million years. Also, as far as I'm aware, he's only stealing food, and though this is rude, it makes me feel sorry for him. He's obviously living rough in the forest. He's hungry, plus, he saved my life. Also, under all the dirt and hair and bad clothes, he's bloody gorgeous.

"Owen, let him get out. He's the one who rescued me, give him a break," I say. "He won't be back."

"No way," says Owen.

I stand back and watch the show. I don't rate Owen's chances. The intruder is slim, young and as bouncy as a professional high jumper. Owen launches himself across the room, and the toaster, a row of immaculate cookery books and Mother's new IKEA-standard lamp all crash to the floor. Now Owen is blocking the doorway. He fishes out his mobile and stabs the buttons with his thumb, never taking his eyes off the boy, who is holding a chair in front of him.

"You're not going anywhere," he says. He speaks into his phone. "Got him," he says. "Get to my place, now."

"Who are you talking to?" I ask from my position curled up in the window seat.

"Go to bed, Lexi," snarls Owen. "He's dangerous."

"No he's not," I say. "He's just a kid. Let him go."

"Are you stupid? He's trying to rob us," says Owen, through gritted teeth.

I shrug. "So why don't you call the police?" I think Owen has phoned up one of his vile mates and they'll probably take great pleasure in beating him up. Imagine if it was Devlin here, cowering under Owen's meaty fists. We all stare at each other for a few minutes. Nobody trusts anybody. The boy isn't smiling now; he looks scared, and I don't blame him.

"Go upstairs, Lexi," roars Owen finally.

"I can't," I say. "You're in the way."

Owen steps aside to let me pass but I don't move.

"Lexi!" bellows Owen again. Then there is a quiet knock at the door.

"That was quick," I remark. "Who says you can never get hold of a policeman when you want one?" But I know it isn't a policeman out there.

"Go and answer the door, Lexi," says Owen slowly. "Then go to bed." He's trying very hard not to lose his temper. I don't want to do it. I don't want to let in some thug to beat up this trampy boy.

"I'm going to call the police," I say brightly. I'm trying to keep the atmosphere light because I'm aware it could turn nasty any minute.

"They're on their way," says Owen through his teeth. I have no loyalty to Owen, and I don't care less that this lad is trying to steal some sausages. He saved my life, so I owe him one. I need to create a diversion.

"Here," I call, clicking back the catch and swinging open the window behind me.

"No you bloody don't!" roars Owen and leaps for the window. The boy uses this opportunity to go for the door and I slip round to get between him and Owen. As the boy flies through the door I am hit by a barrage of large sweaty man as Owen smashes into me. "Get out the way, you dumb cow!" he howls. I am knocked to the floor. I grab at his foot and he trips and lashes out at me, catching the side of my head.

"Ouch," I say in a very small voice.

"Owen!"

Through half-closed eyes I see Mother, halfway down the stairs, fishing out an earplug. "What are you doing?" Her voice is harsh. But I am in pain now and I don't care about any of them any more. My head feels swimmy. I may be sick. Being booted in the head was not part of my diversion plan. I shut my eyes and curl up in a ball. Somewhere else there is shouting and swearing and crashes and thuds and glass breaking.

A male voice shouts, "In the garden."

Then there's a loud crack, like a gunshot, and a high-pitched yell. Doors bang and I hear running feet and cars revving their engines. Then it's quiet.

All except a panicky voice.

"*Lexi, Lexi?*"

Ugly Day

"You let him get away." Owen is furious with me but I don't care. It's 3 a.m. and I'm lying on the sofa with a wet cloth on my sore head. Mother put it there.

"You kicked her," she says icily. She's sitting next to me on the sofa. The side of my head is swollen and I'm going to have a bruise. I am going to look like a rough, fighting girl. I'm also worried about what may have happened to the boy. One of the triplets, Lucas, was here briefly, but Mother sent him away pretty fast.

"It was an accident," snarls Owen. "She deliberately tried to trip me. Didn't you?"

"Yes," I say, and shut my eyes against the pain.

"Lexi," says Mother, shocked. "What were you playing at?"

"The burglar saved my life, you know, up at Beacon House Hospital. Same bloke," I say weakly. I raise myself on my elbows and glare at Owen. "Did you shoot him?"

"Of course not," he says, exchanging glances with Mother. "You heard Lucas's car backfiring." My head goes all swimmy and I fall back down on to the sofa. I feel my eyes filling up with tears. It seems I'm not very

good at getting kicked in the head and being all cheery afterwards.

There's a silence.

"Why was Lucas Neasdon here?" Mother asks Owen. I've never heard her speak to him like this. "Why didn't you call the police?" I don't look at him. The smell of his sweat is overpowering.

Owen swears. "We could have got some information out of him, Paula," he says. "About your dog. He might know something." Even in my misery I can't help but admire Owen for that one. But it's not enough.

"How dare you hurt my daughter," says Mother. And I nearly pass out in shock. I must be hallucinating. She's actually sticking up for me.

"She let him go!" bellows Owen. He looks like he wants to land another one on me and I shut my eyes.

"Stay away from her," hisses Mother.

I should record this and play it to myself every time I feel hard-done-by. "Go to bed, Lexi," she orders. I sit up, wrap the blanket round me, and go. I drift off to the sound of raised voices.

In the morning my head hurts, and sure enough, I have a bruise on the side of my forehead. Owen could have killed me! I feel a bit shaky, and my legs are stiff, like I've been running. I creep downstairs and out the back door. I step into the wet grass in my bare feet and scour the ground. Nothing. I cross the lawn and examine the back fence. Then I see it – a scrap of red material

hooked on a splinter of wood. I stand on a plant pot and look over the fence at the narrow path between the back gardens. There are dark-red splashes of dried blood on the paving stones. Oh God! Did Owen get hold of the boy after all? What should I do? As ever, the sight of blood makes me feel dizzy and sick. I jump down and go back inside the house. Mother is up, bustling round the kitchen. I prepare myself for another showdown. But I'm all worked up for nothing. Mother tells me Owen was called away early this morning and won't be back until tomorrow.

"He was supposed to be working on the Agruba removal," she says. "But he was taken off the job at the last minute. That's why he came home. Otherwise we'd have been alone with the thief."

I look away. Obviously after what happened last night I'd rather Owen had been flying off to Africa with Nyasha Agruba than laying into me.

Mother hands me a cup of tea. "Owen said to say sorry." I raise my eyebrows. I don't believe her, but in a twisted kind of way it's nice that she thought she should lie to me. I tell her about the dried blood and she looks at me like I'm mad.

"Nobody hurt anybody," says Mother firmly. "Owen couldn't catch him."

I take the day off work and spend most of it worrying about the boy. I hope he's OK but I don't know how I'll find out.

The following day I'm hanging around in the

kitchen, looking for something to eat and avoiding the sitting room because Owen's in there watching a programme on TV about the downfall of Britney Spears, when Mother orders me out of the house to buy milk. She says she wants calm so she can order the wedding cake. I slouch out of the house and see a flower lying on the doorstep. It's a black rose. I've never seen one that colour before. I pick it up and it bites me, a thorn bedding into my thumb. I suck at the welling of blood. Then I hold the flower to my nose. It smells fantastic, rich and delicate. I wish I smelled like that.

"Where'd did you get that?" Mother comes up behind me, wrapped up in her white silk dressing gown. She takes the flower from me. "How sweet." She gives a puzzled look in the direction of the sitting room.

"It looks like it's been nicked from a garden," I say, pointing to the twisted-off stem.

"Get the milk," orders Mother, firmly shutting the door in my face and taking the flower with her. I look at the letter box thoughtfully for a few seconds, then nip round the front to eavesdrop under the living-room window.

Did you leave this for me?

Pause.

What? How about another cup of tea, Paula?

"Ha," I say out loud, and go get the milk. I think the flower was left for me, and I'm pretty sure I know who it's from.

Later that day I walk round to Emily Prior's. Visiting

old ladies is about all I'm up for. And when I get there I find her resting on her sofa. The mess is piled up around her and I hate to say it, but she smells a bit. She needs a bath. She's also wearing her old hideous pink lipstick, but I pretend not to notice.

"How's the leg?" I say gaily.

"Not wonderful, dear," says Emily. "The doctor says I need to rest it."

"I tell you what, I'll whip the hoover round if you like," I say, surprising myself.

"There's no need for that," says Emily stiffly. "I can manage quite well, thank you."

"You can pay me in biscuits," I say. "Go on, let me. I love hoovering."

"Really?"

"Is it under the stairs?"

I end up vacuuming the whole of the downstairs, and I clean the kitchen up a bit. Emily stops protesting after a while. We both know it needs to be done and she ends up telling me all about her childhood growing up on a farm. I tell her about the burglar and she goes very quiet.

"But did he really get away?"

I nod. "I think so, but don't worry, I don't think he's dangerous. I think he's the same man who saved my life up at the hospital. I want to find him to see if he's OK. Owen was pretty rough." I don't mention the blood on the path or the rose.

Emily takes a sharp intake of breath and swings her

legs off the sofa and on to the carpet. She looks up at me.

"Don't try to find him," she says, and I'm surprised at the firmness of her voice. "Lexi, dear, I really think it would be best if you left all this alone."

"Why?" I ask.

Emily straightens her skirt. "You're a young girl, Lexi; you shouldn't go out looking for burglars. Who knows what you'll get yourself mixed up in."

This is a good point. But I'm not going to follow her advice.

That evening, Mother suggests we start opening the wedding presents, which have been arriving ever since The Announcement. Owen isn't interested, so Mother and I peel silver paper from bales of peach-coloured towels, pull pink paper ribbons from plastic picture frames and grimace at each other when we unwrap the fourth set of salt and pepper pots. Mother rips the paper from an ornamental doll dressed in purple lace and tries to give the hideous thing to me. I decline. Mother's been sent all sorts of crap: decorative bowls, cutlery, bizarre cooking implements and a lot of "craft" pottery. Mother stacks the cards on the mantelpiece. She says she doesn't want to display them because it's too soon. We find a blue squishy object, which I discover is supposed to be placed in the microwave and then on your forehead. It's supposed to ease headaches. Mother and I actually have a laugh together about this.

"So what would be a good wedding present?" I ask her. "You don't like any of them so far."

Mother thinks for a moment or two. "Guaranteed marital happiness," she says. She looks away. "And I'd love to see Tyson again."

I look down.

"I'm sorry about Tyson," I say, though it nearly kills me. I'm not very good at saying sorry.

"Me too," says Mother. "Me too."

The next afternoon Mother goes to a car boot sale in Charleston and flogs every single present. She comes back with a fistful of fivers and a big smile and says now she can get what she really wants, and is sure deep down, people won't mind. I hope no one finds out. It's a bit cold-hearted even for me. She could at least have waited until after the wedding. But something seems to be happening between me and Mother. OK, we're not exactly sobbing in each other's arms or having cosy chats about life. And God forbid if she ever told me she loved me. In fact, she's almost as much a cow as ever.

Almost.

But the night we got broken into definitely marks The Turning Point. I don't know why seeing me with my head kicked in should make her feel differently about me, but it has. It's like the edge has gone out of her dislike for me. Twice I have turned round and seen a Look Of Concern on her face. And a few times she has begun to have a go at me for something, then stopped herself. She's also given me some cash for some new shoes.

Of course, predictably enough, I blow it.

It's a Thursday afternoon in the last week in August. Owen is at work. Mother is making lists at the kitchen table and I am moodily looking at the horrible food in the cupboards. How am I supposed to snack on Ryvita and diet milkshakes? I consider going over to see Emily, to see if she needs any shopping done. She can't get to the shops at the moment so she is reliant on her neighbours and Meals on Wheels deliveries to stop her from starving.

Mother puts down her pen.

"Lexi, will you be our witness?" I don't recognize the look on Mother's face. She's not meeting my eye. If I didn't know her better, I'd say she was acting a bit shy.

"Witness what?" I say. Does she mean the break-in? I'm not sure I want to give evidence against my rescuer.

"At our wedding."

That sets me back. Witness? Me? She's asking me? Talk about inner turmoil. She's offering me a role in her wedding. She's implying that I am an important person to her. This is weird, but nice. She's trying to build bridges. But she's marrying Owen. He's not right for her. He's not right for anyone.

"Sorry, but no," I say.

I'm not a hypocrite. I'm sad to say it, but I can't happily wave my mother off down the aisle with that animal.

"Right," says Mother. She does not ask me why, or attempt to persuade me otherwise. Surely she can see why I've said no.

"I probably have to be eighteen anyway. . ." I begin, but it is too late. She has collected up her lists and gone. I feel bad. She was reaching out to me and I turned her away. It might not happen again. But I was right not to be a hypocrite, wasn't I? And later, at work, when I discuss the matter with Ella, to my surprise she sides with Mother.

"I know how much you hate Owen, Lex," she says. "I'm not keen on him myself. But the wedding's about your mother, not you and your mad vendetta."

Ouff. Ella certainly doesn't beat around the bush. Usually I like her for it, but now I feel put out. This is because I think she may be right.

It's night-time, and I'm awake again. It's three in the morning. I hate this time of night. It's so late, but nowhere near morning. It's like I'm lost in the night and the day will never come. I'm worrying, worrying, worrying about Mother and me, worrying that I've messed up big time. What's the matter with me? Usually I couldn't care less what Mother thinks. Now I'm working myself into a frenzy about it. I hear something and wonder if Mother is moaning in her sleep. But it's too weird for that. I'm suddenly wide awake and I find myself climbing out of bed and going to the window.

The dogs are howling again. I remember what Owen

said about there being hunting kennels not too far away. I suppose all the villagers are used to the noise, but it freaks me out. I stand there for a while, listening and watching the darkness. I make myself go back to bed, but I can't sleep. The noise is keeping me awake. Bloody animals! I hate not being able to sleep, though admittedly, I'm not as obsessive about it as Mother.

I'm woken at six a.m. by the milkman clanking his bottles. I give up on sleep. Today is going to be an ugly day. I wait until eight o'clock, then phone Ella.

She answers promptly. I'd half expected her to be in bed.

"I want to go up to Beacon Hospital," I say, quietly, in case Owen is listening in. "But I'm too scared to go on my own. Can you come with me?"

"Not today, babe," answers Ella, yawning. She's going shopping with some mates, and she tries to persuade me to come too, and I'd love to. But I can't. I'm going to find the boy, make sure that he's all right, and see if he has Tyson. I think finding Mother's dog would be the best wedding present I could give her. And I want to do something right for a change.

"You must be loopy, going up there again," says Ella. "Wait till Thursday and I'll come with you. It's not safe on your own. What if the mad dogs find you first?"

"I'll take a stick," I say. "Besides, Bewlea Forest is enormous. People must go walking there all the time, and nobody else seems to have had any problems." I hope I sound more confident than I feel.

"So what makes you think you'll find burglar boy?" asks Ella. "And how do you know he's in the forest, anyway?"

"I don't," I say. "But I'm going to try."

Ella also makes me promise to phone her when I get back so she knows I'm safe.

Before I leave, I pack Owen's breakfast sausages into a rucksack. I take a penknife from the kitchen drawer and steal Mother's posh mobile phone from her handbag. She says it gets reception everywhere. It will be useful if I get into difficulties. I'm out of the house before anyone is up. And although I can feel the tiredness in my skin and my eyes, I feel pumped full of adrenaline. I borrow Mother's old bike from the shed so I can make a quick escape from any ferocious dogs.

Mother's bike is purple and the handlebars have tape peeling off them. The tyres feel a bit soft, but I can't remember how to pump them up, and anyway, the extra work will be good for me. I haven't ridden a bike for years. It's not very dignified, but I could get into it. I wouldn't want to wear cycling shorts, though. Nobody looks good in them.

Lunatic

I must be mad to come back here. I'm pushing the bike up the drive, through the forest, to Beacon House Hospital. I should have gone shopping with Ella. Tyson could be anywhere; he could even be dead, for all I know, and despite my bravado earlier, I'm afraid of the other dogs finding me. I look around at the trees as I pad past. I think the boy lives up here, probably in part of the hospital somewhere; otherwise how would he have found me in the cellar? Suddenly everything seems too quiet. I get a prickly feeling on the back of my neck and look round at the trees. Is someone watching me?

"Hello," I call. "Are you there?"

Nothing.

"Thanks for the flower."

Look at me, anyone watching would think I was talking to the trees! Then I see them: the tall dark walls of the asylum. For a minute I feel like I've been transported back in time, and beyond me is a big hospital full of mad people. Maybe I'd have a job here, in the kitchens. I'd boil up vats of vegetables for the inmates. There might be crazy screaming in the background. I look up at the large square clock tower. The

115

hands are stuck at five to three, frozen in time. The main gates are padlocked and, like before, the place appears deserted. I look at the lower windows and shudder. I nearly died in there. My ghost would join all the others.

I push the bike under a bramble bush, but now I'm fast losing the urge to go through the fence. I'm nervous about the dogs. If they come for me, I plan to chuck Owen's sausages at them. I'm about to chicken out altogether and go home when I remember Mother. She'd be so pleased if I found Tyson. I don't have to go in the main house; I'll just look around outside, see if I can find any clues.

I crawl through the fence. I don't think I appreciated last time how huge this place is. The whole complex is immense: outbuildings and sheds, houses and collapsing walls. I pass ruined houses, barns and workshops. I peek through rotting doorways. Some buildings have concrete floors and some are completely overgrown. I walk down broken garden steps to a wide expanse of wild weed and scrub. This could have been a lawn. I turn to look back at the main building. It's a sprawling S shape, with tall chimneys and gated courtyards, waist high with brambles and nettles. I imagine all sorts of holes and coal chutes waiting to transport me back into the cellars. I tread carefully, and in the space of five minutes, I see a rat slinking over a broken drain-pipe, two buzzards circling overhead, and a nosy robin that hops from twig to wall to ground, following me. A large bush grows out of the side of an outhouse. Some of the outbuildings look as if they are held together with ivy. I realize I'm enjoying myself, poking around in the afternoon sun, despite my nerves about the dogs. I find the rusting bonnet of what might have been an army jeep half buried in a vast thatch of stinging nettles. I also find rubbish from when it was a detention centre; old computer monitors stacked against a wall, a dumped carpet, a crate of broken crockery and a cylinder of wire fencing woven with brambles.

The afternoon sun is warm on my face. There's a gap in the trees through which I can see for miles and miles. I can even see a bit of Bewlea village. Why is everyone so mad down there? Moz would say it was because it was on a ley line or something. The vibes have turned everyone's heads. But of course, I don't go in for that sort of stuff.

I turn to go back to the hospital when I step on something soft and smell something rich and flowery. I've trodden on a rose. A red one. I swear it wasn't there when I passed this way a few minutes ago It's been twisted off at the stem.

"Hello?" I call nervously. Further on, on the steps, I see another rose. I go to pick it up. Now I have two red roses. I feel a bit silly.

"Where are you?" I say. I know he is round here somewhere, because, just perceptibly, I think I can smell him.

"Hello."

I step back, because all of a sudden, he's standing in front of me, like he's come out of the ground. He's at least six feet tall, and better-looking than I remembered but dirtier than ever. He smells of b.o. and smoke. There's also a patch of dried blood flaking off his leg.

"Did he hurt you?" I ask, forgetting all about Tyson. "Are you OK?"

The boy smiles. He has amazing teeth, despite one of the front ones being missing. I quite like the look. I realize he's shaking and I'm not nervous any more. He's more scared than I am.

"I'm Lexi," I say. And smile at him. He looks puzzled. "Lexi," I repeat. "My name." Oh no, I hope he's not deranged. But then he smiles back. He looks all around as if he's checking no one is watching. He tries to say something but it's like he's got something stuck in his throat. When he finally speaks his voice is as raw and harsh as my old granddad's, who used to smoke eighty ciggies a day.

"Kos," he says.

Kos

Kos is shy. I'm here asking him all these questions
like, Where do you live? Where is your family? How
did you know to find me? But he doesn't say a word, just
nods and grins. He's leading me through the brambles
and weeds towards the west side of the house. My heart
is racing. Kos really is quite fit, with broad shoulders and
a long back and nice legs, though they're rather on the
thin side. It's a shame he's so dirty. I never was one to go
for the crusty look. I picture him with a haircut and in a
nice pair of jeans and a clean white top. Hmmm.

"Where are we going?" I ask as we climb steps up to
a small door. Kos flashes another of his grins and pushes
it open. I hesitate before going in. Understandably, I'm
not keen to enter. It's a kind of lobby area with high
ceilings and rows of benches against the walls. The floor,
though carpeted with pigeon crap and plaster from the
walls, appears to be made of stone. The place is dark
and wet and stinks of wee and God knows what else.
There are spiders everywhere: little tiny black ones
scurrying over the floor, spindly long-legged creatures
spinning on the walls, and big, evil monsters with hairy
legs. I'm not afraid of spiders, but I don't like them.

"Nice pad," I say.

Kos blinks at me and leads me through a set of doors that once would have had glass in them but now are just empty panes. I'm wondering about this speech thing. I'm finding it weird. "Can you talk properly?" I ask. I know this is not very polite, but this strikes me as essential knowledge. Kos looks at me uncomprehendingly, and the penny drops. "Are you English?" I ask. He looks puzzled. "English?" I repeat.

"No," says Kos, and he looks sad. "Lexi," he says. Then he points to his mouth. "Food?"

"No, I'd taste horrible," I say, realizing that now I'm really confusing him. We're walking through a narrow, dark corridor. It smells old. I'm nervous about the floor and tread exactly in Kos's footsteps.

"I've brought you some sausages, though," I say.

He stops dead. "Sausages?" He says it like this: *suesageees.*

"Kos, who are you?" I ask. But he is not to be led from the subject of sausages.

"Food? Sausages?"

"Meat," I say. "From a pig."

His eyes grow wide.

"Look." I show him the pack of bangers. Kos delicately reaches over for the meat with his grime-encrusted fingers. "I'll cook them," I say, twisting away. I don't want food poisoning, thank you very much. "Where's the kitchen?"

This is what I think about Kos. He's not in his

120

twenties; he's in his late teens. He was or is part of a crew of European travellers, and he's fallen on hard times. Any minute I expect him to introduce me to some more of his buddies, all with equally questionable personal hygiene. From the way he keeps looking at me, I also get the impression he hasn't got a girlfriend. We come out into a wide corridor, and to my alarm, Kos begins climbing a wooden staircase. It looks pretty dodgy; half the treads are missing and most of the banister lies broken on the floor.

"Is that safe?" I ask, following him anyway.

"Safe," says Kos, slurring the word like he can't get his tongue in the right place. But then he smiles again; oh my God. He is the most beautiful man I have ever seen.

Such potential.

"So how come you've been stealing from old ladies in the village?" I ask conversationally as we climb the stairs.

"I was hungry," says Kos, to my amazement. So he can speak and he does understand me. I keep close to the wall, where the wood is double thickness. Kos leads me into a large, light room full of old metal bed frames. Relics, I suppose, from when the place was a hospital. The sunlight streams in through the dusty, broken windows and the floorboards creak when I walk over them.

"It's not exactly homely," I say. Kos fiddles with something in the fireplace and I wander over to see what he's up to. He's made a fire. Grey ashes smolder gently, going red as he blows on them.

He gets up and jumps on a chair leg, making the whole floor shake. He breaks off the leg and shoves it in his fire. Then he kneels and blows again until orange flames spring up. Then he finds a wire tray and places it on the heat. I give him the sausages and watch as he places all six on his griddle. Then he laughs and leans over and kisses my cheek.

This is not how I imagined my first kiss with him. But it will do. I never thought I'd seduce a man with a packet of sausages, but it takes all sorts. I sit on an upturned metal filing cabinet, swinging my legs and tapping the sides with my heels. When the food is ready, Kos eats three sausages straightaway. Then he gives me two (I wrap them in a tissue to soak up the excess grease) and eats the last one himself. I eat one sausage and it tastes amazing. I hand Kos my other one, wrapped in tissue, and watch as he scoffs it down, tissue and all. Then he laughs and kisses me again.

"I love you," he says. It is the first proper sentence I've heard him say. He's got an accent but I can't place it. He laughs and I laugh too. I'm having fun with this crazy guy. I hope I'm not going to fall in love with him. He's not really suitable. I have no intention of running off into the woods with him. It's just not me. I look at the bed nearest me. The springs are all rusting and one of its legs is missing. There's a thick leather strap bolted to the side of the bed. I look away. I know what that is.

It's a restraint, used to tie the mad people down. I dread to think what has gone on in this room in the past.

"Have you got my mother's dog?" I ask, picking at the peeling paint on the filing cabinet.

Kos looks at me under his eyelashes.

"Yes," he says. This is fantastic news. I picture myself bringing Tyson back into the house and handing over his lead to Mother.

Hi, Mum, here's one present you won't be taking to the car boot sale.

I wait, expecting Kos to produce Tyson from somewhere. But he just watches me without saying anything.

"So, can I have him back?" I ask eventually.

"No," says Kos.

"Oh." I stare at him, confused. Is he joking? "Why not?"

Kos goes over to the window and looks out. He turns back to me.

"He's mine now," he says. I don't know if I like him any more.

"Kos," I say firmly. "He's my mother's dog. She wants him back. She misses him."

"Pah," says Kos. "He cry all day with your mother. I hear." Kos smacks his hand on the wall and I jump. "Now he dance. Look." Kos puts his mouth to a hole on the glass and blows out a long sigh. Then he whistles a long, high, breathy note. "Come," he says, beckoning for me to go to the window. I slide off the filing cabinet and join him, treading carefully over the floorboards. I try to look through the window but it's all smeary and I can't see anything.

"Here," says Kos, pointing to a crescent-shaped hole in the glass next to where he's standing. So I stand next to him, conscious how close we are. I'm looking at a grassed-over courtyard enclosed by a tumble-down stone wall, with a wide gateway at the far end.

"What am I supposed to be looking at?" I ask a bit grumpily. I'm still in shock that he said I couldn't have Tyson back. Something is moving in the far corner; I watch as a small spaniel scrambles through a hole in the wall and leaps into the centre of the courtyard. Then he crouches, like he's waiting. Another dog, a terrier, wriggles through the hole and joins the first, lying in the grass. A collie bounds in through the gateway and sits in line next to the others. I recognize it immediately as one of the hounds who tried to eat me.

"Oh Kos," I say. "Is he yours as well?"

Kos touches my arm. "He's sorry."

I grunt, not taking my eyes from the window as the monster dog, followed by an Alsatian, leaps right over the wall into the courtyard and joins the others.

"Did you steal all these dogs?" I ask, knowing it's true.

"Not steal. They leave," says Kos. "They sad before. Shut away all day. Bad owners. Happy with me."

I don't know a great deal about dogs, but I wasn't aware they just ran away from home like some stroppy sixteen-year-old. Yet another dog flies into the courtyard, and I have to grab hold of the window frame for support. It's Tyson, looking thinner but livelier than I've ever seen him. He squats on his belly next to the others, thumping his tail, and they all look up like they're awaiting orders.

"You should be in the circus," I mutter, and Kos gives me a look, making me wonder if I've hit on something.

He whistles again, this time a series of short, sharp noises like *peep peep peep*, and I blink as I watch the dogs get up one by one and run a few metres, then lie down again.

"How have you brainwashed these animals?" I ask, only half in jest.

Kos grins. "My father, he knew dogs. Teach them. I teach them too."

"Why do you keep them all here?"

Kos watches his dogs, now just playing and scratching and sniffing around the yard.

"My friends," he says softly. "My pro ... my protection." He looks at me. "My family. Dogs are special to me and I am special to dogs."

This is all very interesting and I'm impressed, despite my feelings about canines in general. However, now I have Tyson in my sights, I'm not going to let him slip away, no matter what Kos says.

"Tyson!" I yell out of the window. Tyson looks up and cocks his head.

"I have to take him home," I say.

Kos shrugs. "He won't go."

"We'll see about that," I say.

Kos doesn't try to stop me. He follows me back downstairs and even shows me the door to the courtyard outside. I step outside hesitantly, knowing Kos is just behind me but not keen on meeting up with my old doggie chums from a few weeks ago.

They all prick up their ears when they see me, and the collie growls.

"Shhh," says Kos.

"Tyson, come here, boy," I call. But he doesn't even look at me, just carries on licking his paws.

"Tyson, sausages. . ."

But he won't come near me, and I'm not quite brave enough to wade through all those hounds to go up to him. I stand there, sunshine beating down on my head, not knowing what to do, when Kos whistles, so quietly I can barely hear it. At once Tyson leaps up and bounds over. He snakes up to Kos and licks his palm. Then he crouches at his feet, looking up adoringly. As for me, it's as if I'm not here.

"Tyson, you faker, come home with me." I go to put a hand on his neck when he locks eyes with me and emits a low, savage growl.

"Tyson?"

The growling deepens. I don't think I'm going to be taking him home today. I need a lead, and dog food, and maybe even Mother.

"Tyson, you mad mongrel," I say, and I swear he looks confused for a split second before he starts growling again. It's like he's erased all memories of his life with us. He's only been gone for about three weeks. Now he's a stranger. But then again, Tyson never was very easy-going. He'd have a mad look in his eyes even as Mother was strapping him into his tartan jacket.

"Maybe next time," I say, withdrawing. I turn to Kos. "I'll come back tomorrow," I say. "Bring you more sausages. Can I come before work? About ten? I could meet you in the gardens?" I have no idea if he understands me.

Kos grins. There's so much I want to know, like where's he from, and how does he survive? But he's not exactly bursting to tell me.

"Kos, you've got to let me have my dog back," I say, watching as Tyson runs back to join the other dogs. "Can I bring my mother up here?" I ask. "Then you'll see how much she loves him."

But Kos frowns and puts a finger to his lips. "Lexi, Kos, dogs, all secret," he says. "Please."

"Why?" I ask.

"I have enemies," Kos says. "Bad enemies."

I assume he's talking about the people whose houses he's burgled. After all, he's getting a bit of a name for himself. Quite a few people think there is some kind of thieving tramp living up here. He needs to be careful.

"Why do you live like this, anyway?" I ask. "Why don't you live in a house, get a job?"

"Lexi, shhh." Kos puts his finger over my lips. I gently remove his hand. I'm not one for being silenced.

"You're a bit of a mystery man, aren't you?" I say in a flirty kind of way. Kos just shrugs.

"Lexi, please." Kos looks at me from under his lashes. "I hide from everyone but you."

There's a silence, and my stomach gives a leap. In a funny kind of way, there is some chatting up going on here.

"All right, I won't say anything," I say. "For now. But Kos, where are your real family?"

Kos pats his chest, over his heart.

"Dead," he says.

Rabbits

"Did you find him, then?" asks Ella that night as she swings past with a tray of napkins and clean cutlery, ready to set the tables for tonight's meals.

"No," I say. "It was stupid to go up there. I don't know what came over me."

"You should have come shopping with us," she calls going out into the restaurant. Maybe she's right. I don't know what I'm getting myself into here. Kos appears to be homeless, and he doesn't speak much English, and I don't see how he's going to sort himself out as long as he keeps thieving from people. Why doesn't he go to social services and ask for help? He could at least get himself a little bedsit. Then he could get himself a job, and then he'd be warm and safe at night, and...

"Lexi," says Ella, returning with an empty tray. "What is it with you?" She looks at me closely. "You've got ever such bright eyes," she remarks suspiciously. She leans closer. "What are you hiding?"

"Nothing," I say innocently.

"You're not in love, are you?" She winks at me and gestures to Jak, who is scrubbing oven trays.

"No," I say much too quickly. "Of course not." I'm

filling up the salt cellars. I've got sixteen to do, and after that I've got to fill sixteen tomato sauce dishes, but my mind's not on the job.

"You made a mess." Jak is beside me, pointing at the salt sprinkled all over the table. "Let me help you." He takes the carton of salt from me and begins pouring it into a cellar.

I look at him sideways. "Haven't you got your own work to do?" He's been following me around ever since I got here this evening. Even Ella has noticed.

"He can't leave you alone," she whispers, gliding past with her empty tray. "Bet he tries to snog you later."

It's not easy when someone fancies you. You've got to let them down gently so they don't get mad or sad. You've got to be careful you don't lose a mate. I hope Jak doesn't make A Declaration.

"Ella says you went into the woods," says Jak suddenly. "Do you want me to come with you next time? Aren't you scared of the dogs?"

God! He's a pain.

Ella winks.

"It's not the dogs I'm scared of," I mutter into the massive jar of tomato sauce.

I'm bursting to tell Ella about Kos. But Ella really can't keep a secret and if I tell her, she'll tell her mum, and then the whole village will know in twenty-four hours.

"Come on now, Jak," I say brightly. "Are you stalking me or what?"

He blushes. "No, no, it's just. . ."

"I like walking in the woods on my own," I say. "I get a buzz out of nature, you know? I like to meditate with the trees." Out of the corner of my eye I can see Ella is killing herself trying not to laugh. "But thanks," I say. I put my hand on his wrist and he jumps like I've electrocuted him. Later I swipe a bowl of chips for him because he's looking a bit low and he brightens up. I only hope he doesn't think they are love-chips. . .

The next morning, I find myself back in the "gardens" of Beacon House Hospital. I bought some food from the post office store. I've also got Tyson's lead in my bag and a packet of doggy chocs I found in the cupboard. I'm hoping to persuade him to come home with me, though after yesterday, I don't rate my chances. As I was walking up the lane to the hospital, I thought I saw something move through the trees ahead of me. I don't know for sure, but I think it was one of Kos's dogs. I'm wondering if he has trained them to do other things than just run about and sit down. I'm wondering if he uses them like some kind of *patrol*. I don't know if such things are possible. I remember being in a history lesson where the teacher was talking about dogs being used to send messages in wars, and there are guide dogs and sniffer dogs, of course. But maybe there are loads of other things that dogs can be trained to do.

I'm crawling through the hole in the fence when I

realize something. It's so awful I stop moving, unable to comprehend how this could have happened. I put my hands on my face. The skin feels soft, but bare.

I forgot to put any make-up on this morning! This is unheard of. Make-up has been a major part of my life since I was at least seven years old. No! I sit up, and try to think how this could have happened. I remember picking out my nice soft grey T-shirt. It hugs me in all the right places and I wanted to look good because I was coming to find Kos (not that I'm planning to pull him, of course). Usually I put my make-up on before I come downstairs, but today I sneaked down early to raid the food cupboard before anyone was up. Then I lay low until everyone was out, slipped into the shed to get Mother's bicycle, and came out here, obviously forgetting my usual beauty routine. I feel naked! I debate going home. I don't want Kos to see me like this; he'll go right off me. I haven't even got any eyeliner on! But then I squeal as I feel a hand on my shoulder. I look up to see Kos grinning at me. Too late to go home, then. Kos looks pretty pleased to see me despite my lack of war paint. Or maybe he's just being polite. Hmm. He has a good chin, despite the straggly boy-beard, and his shoulders and arms are lush. I feel myself melt. Lexi, I tell myself, you can't fall for this man. He is NOT SUITABLE. It was hard leaving Chas Parsons; he was cute and he made me laugh. But he was trouble. He was Devlin's best mate, and he had no morals. I decided after Chas, I would only go out with men who weren't lawbreakers. I would date normal lads, with cars and jobs, who maybe played football on a Saturday, not went out joyriding and looking for trouble. But here I am making eyes at *Stig of the Dump!* I need my head examined.

"Food?" Kos asks.

I smile. At least he's straightforward. I hand him a packet of chocolate biscuits from my bag and watch as he demolishes them. I decide that, even though I must look awful, I'll just forge on and hope he is dazzled by my beaming personality.

"Where do you sleep?" I ask. "Up a tree?"

Kos wipes chocolate crumbs from his mouth. How am I going to get him to take a bath? Could I smuggle him home somehow and lock him in the bathroom? He gestures for me to follow him and we pick our way through the undergrowth. We go round the back of the main house. Kos walks with confidence, like he hasn't got a care in the world. I'd have expected him to be more cautious. I step on a pane of glass half-embedded in the ground, and the cracking noise echoes off the walls. Kos drops to the ground, like he's scared of being shot. Maybe he's not so relaxed after all.

"It's only me," I say, and he gets up. We walk away from the main building and down a gentle slope to a high hedge. Behind this are several small outhouses.

Kos grins at me and pushes the door of the first one. The door is stiff, like no one has opened it for a long time. Inside it's dark and smells musty, like charity shop clothes. (I am not a fan of dead people's clothes but Moz is always trying to drag me round the second-hand shops in Bexton.) The shed is just one big room inside, with narrow benches lining the walls. The floor is littered with food wrappings and drink cartons. There's a mattress in one corner with the stuffing coming out, and a manky-looking blanket.

"It needs a few home comforts," I say. "Like not being a shed. But I'm sure it has great potential."

"In winter I sleep here," Kos says in his crazy voice.

Kos leads me out of the hut to a gap in the perimeter fence. We squeeze through and head into the forest. I think he understands me better today. And he's coming out with more words. If I were to make a wild guess, I'd say it wasn't that he couldn't talk, but that he was *out of practice.*

We walk through the trees in the sunshine and Kos points to a high branch, where I see a brilliant flash of green as a tiny bird swoops over. Kos shows me lots of other things. A white stone that has crystals inside, a brilliant red fungus, and a fox, sitting frozen in the ferns just below us, watching us with bright eyes. Kos presses a small blue flower into my palm and lifts it to my nose. The smell is very sweet and strong and I rub the flower over my wrists so I'll smell nice all day.

"Lexi."

I look round but can't see Kos anywhere.

"Up, Lexi, up, up."

I look up and see only branches and leaves and a

patch of blue sky. Something small lands in my hair and I tug out an acorn.

"Kos?"

Then I see him, way, way above me, stretched out on a massive branch and gazing down.

"Come," he says.

"Forget it; I'm not a bloody monkey."

"Lexi, you like up here."

"No," I say, craning my neck and wrinkling my eyes. "Lexi like down here."

"Lex-ie," he calls in a cajoling voice, and all at once a rope lands at my feet. It is knotted here and there, with sticks tied in. It's the same rope Kos used to rescue me from the cellar. I look at it and shudder.

"Come ON, Lexi," says Kos. "Lexi scared?"

"No," I snort. But of course I am. I look up at Kos again. I bet he can see for miles. I feel a surge of energy. I could maybe just have a little go; I can stop whenever I want. Why not? It's not like I'm like poor old Emily with a bad leg and pushing eighty. It's time I had some fun. The tree looks climbable. I think it's a beech tree; there was one a bit like it in the playground at my old school.

"All right, then," I say, grabbing the rope. "I'll show you." I heave up on to the first branch and swing round so fast I lose my balance and slip to the ground, thudding on to my bum. It's not far to fall, but I don't feel very dignified. Maybe this wasn't such a good idea.

"Lexi, why you sitting?" Kos laughs at me. So I get up and have another go. This time I rest my feet on the trunk

135

of the tree and haul myself up. I discover a little notch cut into the tree, perfect to slot my foot in. A little higher up, there's another. Kos must have cut these footholds in, but some time ago because the bark has grown over. I keep climbing, and though it is hard work and I'm sweating, it is easier than I'd expected, with my knotted rope and the footholds which appear all the way up the trunk. But Kos is still a long way above me. I grit my teeth and keep going. I really don't know what's come over me. Since I've moved here I've become like a female Tarzan, hanging out with tramps, forgetting to put on my make-up, and climbing trees! Moz would kill herself laughing if she saw me now.

Kos climbs down to meet me. When I see him move I'm not surprised he manages to stay hidden. He moves down the tree effortlessly and gracefully, making it look easy. I used to do gymnastics until quite recently. I did some competitions. I was OK, but I wasn't the best. But Kos reminds me of a top gymnast. He's so sure and confident, and has long, toned muscles, like he uses them every day.

I swing my leg over a fat branch and cling to it, panting. This is when I look down. I've climbed maybe twenty feet.

"That's it," I say. "I'm not going any higher."

Kos steps on to my branch.

"Look," he says, and points.

I curl my legs round the branch and look out over the forest. The trees spread for miles around. I see the pylons stepping down the valley and follow them until I see the purple blur of Bewlea village. Then I look down to the base of the tree. Now I just have to work out how to get down. As I am thinking about this I notice a movement on the ground and see what I think is a dog coming out of a dark recess in the ground. I look harder, holding tightly to the branch. Yes, it looks like a sort of cave, mostly covered over with bracken and dead branches. There's a dip in the ground which leads all the way to a sort of drop. I can't see very well because there are too many trees in the way.

"What's that?" I ask Kos, pointing.

"Secret," he says, pulling his hair back away from his face.

It's difficult getting down. For one thing I'm tired, and also I can see how far I have to fall. The rope cuts into my hands and twice my foot slips from the toeholds. Kos makes it to the ground twice as fast as me. He really is pretty amazing. I wish I were as fit as him. I'm sitting on the ground, examining a new graze on my arm, when I notice that Kos is looking intently at something. I follow his gaze and see a group of three rabbits nibbling grass just a little way off.

"Oh, how cute," I say. "Don't tell me, they're your little forest friends. I bet you speak rabbit language even if you can't speak English. . ." I stop talking. Kos has produced a contraption made of sticks and rubber from somewhere in his clothing. He searches the ground and picks up a stone.

"Kos," I say. "You're not going to. . ." I watch, horrified, as he catapults the stone into the furry group. Then he springs after it. He's hit one, but it's not quite dead. It falls down the bank, thrashing its legs. But then Kos is there, picking it up. With one twist he breaks its neck. He holds it up by his ears and gives the limp body a little victory shake. He grins at me but this time I'm not able to smile back.

I must get back on course. I'm here about Tyson.

"Kos," I begin. "Can you take me to Tyson?"

But before he can answer there's a crackle of breaking twigs and scrunching leaves, and two women stride out of the trees along the path, just a little way off, chatting and laughing. They're in their fifties and wearing walking boots, with thick socks pulled up over their trousers. They have maps in plastic pouches around their necks. I turn to Kos but he's not here any more, nor is the dead rabbit.

I sing as I cycle back. I'm not very good at singing but I love doing it. Especially when I'm in love. No, Lexi, no!

"Where've you been?" demands Mother when I walk in.

"Just out, you know, hanging out with drug dealers and planning a bank robbery." I smile at her.

"You're in a good mood," she says suspiciously.

"We drug dealers are always cheerful," I say. As I take off my jumper, bits of twigs and leaves fall on the carpet. Luckily the phone rings and it must be something to do with the wedding because she forgets I'm there. I eye a bag of groceries on the kitchen counter. I'll have to go through that later, see if there's anything for Kos. And maybe I could find something of Owen's for Kos to wear. I catch myself humming as I go upstairs. I'm up, up, up!

No, Lexi, no!

Mugged

With two weeks to go, the wedding frenzy is mounting. Owen is off on a week-long escort job, hurrah!, and Mother is on a major beauty kick. She's going to the gym every day before work, and the bathroom is full of brand-new lotions and potions. I'm wearing dead expensive perfume, two different sorts of hair mousse, cherry lipgloss, and some really lush foundation which I'd never be able to afford. Luckily, Mother has the same skin tones as me. She's got foot lotions and scrubs for the rough skin on your elbows. She's got new lip-liners and lipsticks. She's got glitter powder, green correction fluid and fat eye pencils of all colours. And more of this stuff appears on the already-loaded bathroom shelves every day. The house is stacked with leaflets about colour schemes and seating arrangements, about two-day detox diets and wedding dress spot treatments. There are packets of glitter spots for scattering on the meal tables and boxes of biodegradable pink confetti in case people forget to bring their own. There's bubble mixture in small plastic containers shaped like wedding cakes, and hundreds of silver balloons waiting to be inflated. I can't help thinking that all this stuff is a bit tacky, really. It's like it's more important than the wedding itself. I worry Mother has got so caught up with the whole idea of the wedding – the dress, the glitter, the show – that she's forgetting what it's really supposed to be about – like making a promise to spend the rest of your life with someone. Mind you, if I were marrying Owen, I'd want to forget about that too.

Mother and Celia are preparing for the hen weekend. Eight of Mother's mates are going to Cornwall to stay in a cottage. They're planning to do all sorts of things, like massages and saunas and beauty treatments. I'd love to do something like that, but in different circumstances. The front room is full of pink fluffy rabbit ears and body glitter and party games. There are crates of wine and boxes of party food. Celia is sorting through a pile of pink T-shirts on the hall table, with PAULA'S HEN written on them in sequins.

"Can I have some money?" I ask. I don't get paid until next week and I'm skint. Otherwise I wouldn't have set foot in the room.

Mother shakes her head. "Sorry, I haven't got anything." She turns her head this way and that in the mirror. "What do you think, Celia?" She's trying on a pink cowboy hat. "Do you think I should order some for everyone?"

"Definitely," says Celia. "You only get married once."

"Or twice in your case," I say. I bite my tongue. When am I going to learn to keep my mouth shut?

Mother looks round at me and I prepare to get an earful.

"Come with us, Lexi," she says. "I'm sure I can clear it with Wendy to get you the time off."

"It will be fun, Lexi," says Celia.

"I'll see," I say, too amazed to think of anything else to say. Is she going soft in her old age? Of course I don't want to go. Don't I? But I really like the idea of a weekend of pampering. *Say yes say yes,* a little voice inside urges me. But all Mother's friends hate me. It would be awful.

I wish things were different.

"I'd better go to work or I'll be late," I say.

Outside it is pouring with rain, and as Mother didn't offer me a lift, I arrive at the hotel soaking wet, with my hair plastered down my face. It's going to dry all frizzy. By the end of the night I'll have hair like Kos's. I think about him as I peel the millionth potato. Where is he sheltering from the rain? Is he is in the Big House, or in his shed? Maybe he's under a tree, surrounded by all his dogs.

"I like your hair," says Jak, coming in with a crate of onions.

"Shut it," I say.

"No, honestly," says Jak. Oh dear. He must fancy me if he likes the look of me in this state. It's busy again tonight and I have to do extra waitressing. I don't mind. It's better than the meat pans. Emily is here with a gang of her old-lady buddies. They come in every fortnight on a Friday for a slap-up meal. Emily waves at me. She's wearing the lipstick I brought her. It looks miles better than the old one. They're all gossiping about how there hasn't been a burglary for two weeks, and it must be because of the petition they sent to the police station about extra policing. As I give them their soup, I notice that Emily is rather quiet. I ask her if she's OK and she smiles and nods and says I must come and visit her again soon. I pop back a few minutes later with another bottle of wine and see she isn't in her chair.

"Where's Emily?" I ask.

"In the ladies'," says Mrs Harris from the post office. "Don't worry about her, dear. She's always like this when one of us has good news."

"Sorry?" I look down at her. Oh man, to think I'm going to be that wrinkly one day. I should start saving up for my facelift now.

"Angie's expecting," says Mrs Harris, pointing to the old biddy next to her, who has a smug look on her face.

"Really?" I look at her stomach, hidden under folds of floral dress. She must be nearly eighty! I thought such things were impossible.

"My fourteenth grandchild," says Angie. "Due at Christmas."

"Emmie always gets upset when there's a grandchild on the way," says Mrs Harris. "She could never have children of her own. Therefore, no grandchildren."

"Right," I say, a tad perturbed at being included in this conversation.

"Here comes Emmie," whispers the fourth woman. I don't know her name but I like her shoes. They're black patent stiletto heels. She's got very long silver hair tied back in a smooth ponytail. Emily sits awkwardly, dropping her stick. I pick it up for her and prop it against the table. Then I top up her wine glass because she looks like she could do with it, though I'm not supposed to because I'm under eighteen. Then I flee back into the kitchen. I thought life got less complicated when you were old. It seems not.

I finish my shift at ten. I have to wait behind because Wendy wants to talk to me about extra hours, but she's rushing around sorting out puddings. Ella is waiting to walk home with me but I wave her on.

"I might be ages, and you need to be in bed," I say, looking at her red nose. She's coming down with a cold. Also I want to nick a few bits of food for Kos and I don't want Ella to see.

I finally get out at twenty past ten. My rucksack is stuffed with a nearly full box of after-dinner mints, half a block of cheese and two pints of milk along with my work clothes. It's stealing, I suppose, but I try not to think about that. I'm walking through the car park. It's not very well lit but I see a couple of people at the far end. It's Ella with a boy. The sneaky so-and-so. . .

"Hey," I call, starting towards them. But something is

wrong. Very wrong. The boy is holding something pointed which glints in the lamp light, and Ella is reaching in her bag. She lets out a sob.

"No!" I yell, outraged, pounding up to them. "Leave her alone."

The boy turns to me, a horrible menacing look on his face. From the look of him, he's got every intention of mugging me as well. Then his face falls. I'm unable to believe what I'm seeing. The boy grins, and before he can say anything, I slap him round the head.

"How dare you mug my mate, you bloody loser!" I stand and scream all the worst names I can think of.

"Lexi, he's got a knife," says Ella nervously. "Don't wind him up."

He's dressed in horrible tracksuit trousers, a nasty white jacket and a dirty baseball cap.

I'm so angry about him robbing my lovely mate, I want to kill him. "NOW PISS OFF," I bellow at him. "Come on, Ella," I say. And I lead her away, out of the car park.

"Shall we go into the hotel?" whispers Ella, looking nervously behind. "It will be safe there."

"Don't worry, you're safe with me," I say grimly.

When we're on the street, she bursts into tears. "Who was that? I haven't seen him before."

"He'd better never come back if he knows what's good for him," I growl.

"Maybe he's the Bewlea burglar," says Ella.

I hesitate. "I don't think so," I say.

"You were amazing," she says. "So brave! Like a mad banshee." I say nothing but squeeze her hand. By the time I've walked Ella home, she's stopped shaking. "You don't think things like that are going to happen in this village," she says.

"No," I agree grimly.

"Should I bother calling the police?" asks Ella. "He's probably long gone by now, and they won't do anything."

I take a deep breath. "It's up to you."

Ella doesn't want to let me go. "It's not safe on your own," she says. "He might come back. Wait here with me until Mum gets home and she'll give you a lift."

"Don't worry," I say, grim-faced. "I'm not scared of anyone." I walk home through the darkness. I want to scream, I want to cry. And after a while I hear footsteps running behind me. "What kind of a low-life scumbag mugs a woman on her own?" I say without turning round. The footsteps get closer. I storm ahead. "You're a disgusting, evil, FAT parasite."

"Lex, I didn't know she was your mate. . ."

"It doesn't make any difference." I stop dead. "You disgust me, Devlin Juby," I yell at my brother. "And what the hell are you doing here, anyway?"

ASBO

My brother lies stretched out on the sofa like he owns the place. He's wearing a new pristine white hoody, doubtless bought with dirty money, and equally new trainers, which are now resting on Mother's sofa. Mother and Owen are out. I didn't want to let Devlin in the house but was worried he'd get into more trouble and everyone would find out he was my brother.

"All right, Lex?" he asks, slurping a low-fat yogurt he's swiped from the fridge.

"No," I snap. I glare at him. "Why do you do it? Why can't you be a human for once?"

Devlin looks puzzled. "I wanted some money."

"Have you had your brain botoxed?" I snarl. "You'll get slammed up if you get caught breaking your ASBO. And I thought you'd sworn to Mother you'd stopped the muggings."

Devlin rolls his eyes. "Oh come off it; don't tell me you've been squeaky-clean since you've been here."

"Yes I have," I lie, thinking of the food in my rucksack. But that's different, isn't it? I slump on the chair. Maybe it's not so different after all. Maybe, in my way, I'm just as bad as Devlin. "How long are you staying?" I ask.

Devlin shrugs. "I only came for a visit; I got it cushy at home. We're having parties every night – you should come back, Lex, we're having a right laugh." He stops. "Place is a bit trashed, though."

I bite my lip. "What?" I say quietly.

"You have spoken to Dad?" Now Devlin looks worried.

"No," I say in a controlled voice. "Dad told me you were staying with Uncle Petey."

"Ah," says Devlin. "Then he hasn't told you yet." He looks at his hands. "Oh dear."

"Told me what?" I get up and stand over him. "TOLD ME WHAT?"

"He said he was going to tell you last week," says Devlin.

"Speak," I say. "Or I'm phoning the police and getting you arrested for mugging my mate. She'll make a good witness. And you'll get locked up for breaking your ASBO."

"Like Dad, then," mutters Devlin, not looking at me.

"What?"

Devlin swings his legs round to sit up. "He said he wanted to be the one to tell you. Oh man, I'm crap at keeping secrets."

"Devlin Juby, what the hell is going on?" I scream. I feel all wobbly, like the floor is falling away from me. Dad, in jail? Is that what Devlin means? "Where's Dad?" I grab his arm. "Tell me."

"In Her Majesty's pleasure," says Devlin. "In Puckington, just outside Bristol. Oops, I shouldn't have said that."

I need to know more. "How long is he inside for, and *what did he do?*"

But Devlin just flicks through the channels. "Tea would be nice. Milk and five sugars, please, Lex."

"You're lying," I say. "Dad would have told me."

The front door opens. Mother and Owen are back. I rush out into the hallway.

"IS IT TRUE ABOUT DAD?" I scream. Mother clocks Devlin's jacket lying on the carpet and instantly knows what I'm talking about.

"I'm afraid it's true, Lexi," says Mother softly. "Your father's in prison. He got sent down last week. He didn't want you to know, just in case he got let off." She puts her hand on my shoulder. "I'm sorry, Lexi; I promised not to say anything because I thought it was better for you."

I shrug her off. "You were wrong," I say.

The rest of the evening is messy. I yell at Mother for not telling me the truth, at Devlin for being a psycho, and at Owen for existing. Now I'm lying on my bed, gazing at Manhattan. It's late. Everyone has gone to bed. Devlin is in the spare room. We're one big unhappy family.

"How long?" I'd screamed at Mother. "How long am I going to be stuck in this dump?"

"He's not due for parole until Christmas," said

149

Mother. Then she told me what he'd done. He'd set up an internet business, flogging off stolen property and lifting people's credit card details when they bought the dodgy stuff.

"And you wonder why she left him," muttered Owen. I lost it properly then. It's embarrassing to think about. When am I going to learn how to keep my cool?

I turn over on my bed. I'm seeing my room with new eyes. I'm going to be here for at least four more months. I get a pang for our scruffy kitchen at home in Bexton. I can't believe Dad didn't tell me about this. I've watched him bend the truth and tell bare-faced lies to loads of people. And I knew there was something odd about the France/wine business, but he's never lied to me like this before.

Things will never be the same between us.

I hear a gentle knock at the door.

"If that's you, Devlin, you can f. . ."

"It's me." Mother pushes open the door. She closes it behind her and stands looking at me. "Lexi, I know this is hard."

"Yes," I say. "It is."

"I think you should know something," says Mother.

I look at her, saying nothing.

"He didn't want you to know because he was ashamed," says Mother. "He couldn't bring himself to tell you. He had his court date and was worried he was

150

going to be sent down. But he hoped he wouldn't."

"Why didn't you tell me?" I ask. I hate that everyone knew except me.

"Lexi, he called me and asked that I keep it from you until he could explain it all to you himself. He didn't want you to hate him."

"I hate him now," I say. "I never want to see him again."

Mother breathes in. "I'm sorry, Lexi. I wasn't sure what to do. In the end I didn't tell you because I wanted to protect you from all the worry. I did it for you."

"Whatever," I say, turning my back on her. If she was a normal mother, this would be the time she gave me a hug, and said everything was going to be OK. But Mother just sighs and leaves the room.

Tears trickle on to my pillow. Down again.

I'm lying in bed at one o'clock and the moonshine streams through my window. I want to do something. I'm feeling reckless now, not sad. What I really want to do is sneak Kos home and make him have a bath. Then I'd like to cook him something fabulous and then maybe have a cuddle on the sofa. I bet he's a wild kisser. But of course I can't just bring him back here. There's Mother, Owen and Devlin, all dreaming their evil dreams just a few feet away. But there's nothing to stop me going to see him. Once the idea is in my head, I can't get it out. I'm not being very sensible but I don't care. I dress in my thin black jumper and black jeans, my trainers and my grey jacket. I put a pack of iced buns (Owen's, of course), a large German sausage and some bottles of beer into my rucksack. I nick a scarf of Mother's because it's quite cold outside, then slip out into the night. I creep into the garage and fetch Mother's bike. I wheel it out into the deserted street.

I pedal fast, zooming through the streets and out into the lanes. I have the feeling that I could keep cycling for ever. There's zero traffic and I'm at the forest in twenty minutes flat. I push the bike up the lane. Thank goodness for the moon, but it's still pretty dark. I try not to think of all the horrible things that might be lurking in the trees.

I pad up the road. The air smells good up here: clean and earthy, though my favourite smell in the whole world is the smell of petrol. I used to love going to fill the car up with Dad at the garage. I'd wind down the windows and just sniff. Or maybe I just loved being out with Dad and the smell was all part of it. I blink back the tears and walk faster.

I remember the first time I found out my dad wasn't exactly kosher. I must have been about eight years old. I'd always worshipped my dad. He was the one who was there for me. He took me shopping for clothes and put food in the cupboards. (He didn't cook it, though; I did that, but he did bring home lots of takeaways.) But one day I was at the garage with him, and this old lady came running up on her shaky old legs, waving her fist and calling him names I'd never have thought a little old lady would know. She was accusing him of ripping off her son over a car. The car had been stolen and traced back to the owner. Dad just ignored the woman and bundled me away. But when I asked him about it, he told me to be quiet.

A year or so later, in the Christmas holidays, I was bored. As always, Dad was out, and we'd had the place to ourselves. I was messing around with Moz, and for some reason we'd ended up in the garage. It was cold in there. For a while we'd sat on some tyres and tried to smoke a fag we'd found in one of Dad's coat pockets. Moz noticed the big blue tarpaulin covering a mound at the back of the garage.

"What's that?" she'd asked. I wasn't very interested. Dad was right into his car boot sales and always had piles of junk lying around. I'm not into junk, I like space, but Moz went over to look. Under the tarp she found a pile of heavy-duty bin bags. I assumed it was rubbish or car boot stuff and didn't fancy looking any further but Moz, being Moz, ripped the nearest one open. Inside we found loads of CDs, and a couple of cameras and even a microphone and lots of technical-looking equipment; we didn't know what that was for. The next bag had a couple of laptops, a leather jacket and computer games.

"What's all this?" asked Moz. I had no idea. But then Devlin came in and told us to clear off out of it. I had no intention of doing so but then he hit me and it was getting cold anyway, so we'd scarpered.

Later, when I'd pestered Dad about it, he said it was

just stuff for a car boot sale. I wanted to go and look through the CDs but he wouldn't let me. And a couple of days later, it had all gone.

It wasn't long before I found out what all that stuff really was.

Every now and then, me and Devlin would have a really massive row. It usually started with something stupid, like us wanting different TV channels (even though we both had TVs in our rooms). Or him picking a fight with me. (Did I mention that my brother has a *major* attitude problem?) The fights usually blew over pretty quick. Dad would come and sort us out or Devlin would start getting violent and I'd run out.

This row, however, was a real blinder.

It started, as ever, for a very small reason. Devlin had wanted a pen, and he'd gone into my room. I hadn't given him permission and I found him rifling through my desk. I'd screamed at him and called him a nosy snooper, or words to that effect, and why did he want a pen anyway because he couldn't even write properly (Devlin never really "got" school) and he'd got mad (he gets mad easily). He'd gone on at me and called me a creep, or words to that effect, and said how I was always brown-nosing Dad. It's too dumb to go over it all, really. Eventually, he'd punched me, and I'd screamed, and Dad had come up, and caught Devlin punching me again (I'd kicked him in between but Dad didn't see that) and Dad gave Devlin a smack, which sent him flying across the room. Minutes later, me and

Dev were sitting on my bed, listening to the front door slam. Dad always went to the pub when he knew he'd gone too far.

"You think he's so wonderful," said Devlin, rubbing his side where Dad had walloped him.

"At least he didn't abandon us," I snapped.

"At least Mum doesn't rob her own neighbours," said Devlin. He gave me a look. At least Mum doesn't batter people. At least Mum doesn't rip her own friends off."

I stared at him. "What do you mean?"

It was then that he told me that Dad made his living from thieving and robbing and flogging off stolen stuff. I was nine, remember, and I thought my dad was the best. I was also a real goody-two-shoes and freaked out if Moz or Devlin lifted a penny chew from the newsagent's. Devlin told me all the stuff I'd found in the garage was from the spate of burglaries in the area that everyone was talking about. And Dad was involved.

"I don't believe you," I'd said. But I knew it was true.

At the time, my mate Moz was finally sussing the awful truth that Father Christmas didn't exist, that he was really her old man dressed up in a Poundland Santa suit. I had to deal with a rather different kind of disappointment.

I found out later what Devlin wanted the pen for. It was Mother's birthday the next day. He'd wanted to write her a card. No wonder he was so touchy.

*

It's too dark. I'm pushing the bike through a bit where the trees overhang the lane, so barely any moonlight gets through.

"KOS . . . KOS." Actually it's quite stupid shouting like this. Anything might hear me. If he doesn't turn up I'll go and look in his sleeping shed. He has to be lurking around somewhere. But what if he's gone off burgling and he's not here? I could be all alone in the forest. I press on and get out of the tree tunnel, but now the moonlight casts spooky shadows on the road. Wind sighs through the leaves and I get a wave of sadness. Why am I standing in this lonely wood looking for a strange boy I hardly know?

But all at once, things get worse.

The Quarry

Monster dog creeps out of the shadows and edges towards me. I flick on my torch and shine it right at him. He looks bigger and meaner than ever and his eyes reflect a reddish glow. I wasn't expecting this. At first I'm more annoyed than scared. I'm so stupid to put myself in this situation again. I'd got complacent about these dogs, and this is my punishment. The dog curls up the fur on its back, its ears flattened, like it's about to pounce, and a ripple of fear moves through me. I edge behind my bike so it forms a barrier between me and the monster. It tilts its head and sniffs and its ears prick up.

"I'm mates with your boss," I say. "So don't try anything."

I've got out of this before, I can do it again. I have a bike and a large sausage.

"You're supposed to be man's best friend, you bloody traitor," I snap. "Kos, where are you?" The bike slides out of my damp fingers and I have to grab to catch it. Any minute, he's going to go for me, and the rest will appear and it will be a feeding frenzy. Sweat runs down my back, even though I'm shivering with cold.

"Kos!" I scream. "Come and bloody rescue me."

It may be wishful thinking, but Monster appears to be backing off. To my disbelief, he wags his tail, turns, and bounds off into the shadows. I wait for a minute to see if he comes back, but he doesn't. I shine my torch on the empty road ahead. I've lost the urge for adventure now. Maybe I should just go home. It's very dark and Monster might be back. I think of Dad, miles away, locked up in a cell, and my eyes fill with tears.

"Lexi."

I point the torch at Kos, who is standing just behind me. How did he know I was here? I swear he uses his dogs like an early warning system. He's wearing a dirty white shirt and a pair of shorts. He's got an old sports bag slung over his shoulder.

"Lexi, sad," he says.

"Don't worry about it," I say.

Kos takes my bike from me and wheels it into the ditch at the side of the road. Then he scoops up my hand and leads me into the forest.

"So what are you going to show me now?" I ask, ducking to avoid a low branch. "Your squirrel-hunting technique?" Kos just grins back at me. He has no idea what I'm on about. We trudge on and on and I feel my spirits rise. If I were out on my own, I'd be terrified, but with Kos here it's quite exciting. I feel like I'm having an adventure. Nobody knows where I am, and I like how Kos doesn't let go of my hand. I take stock. Here I am, Lexi Juby, miles from home at night with a wild boy who can hardly talk, and a pack of insane dogs. If I hadn't had such a bloody awful day, would I be here, wandering around a dark wood with a man/boy I barely know, accompanied by a pack of crazed hounds? But the fact remains, he rescued me from the cellar and I've visited him twice before in the daylight and everything was fine.

I trust him.

It's not as dark as I expected, though I keep a firm hold of Kos's hand. I'm not going to get lost again. We climb steadily uphill, walking between columns of fir trees. Then we step out into a plantation of big leafy trees.

We've been walking for about ten minutes when Kos says, "Look."

It's the cave-like opening I'd seen yesterday from the top of the tree.

"Lexi," says Kos, turning to me. "This is secret, OK?"

"Fine," I say. "Trust me." Kos pushes back some vegetation and we step into the cave.

It's a very narrow space, with steep slate walls, and we have to go in single file. I look up and see a star through the ceiling and realize this isn't a cave at all but a narrow gorge, with a roof of tree roots holding up soil and vegetation. The ground slopes away quite steeply and I feel like I'm going underground.

Eventually we come out into a big open space. I lose my balance and a clatter of stones falls away and Kos holds my arm. I shine my torch around. We're in a massive, deep pit, like a lunar landscape. Steep crumbling walls surround us. I think we're in a quarry. There's a campfire burning a little way off. As we climb down the pile of stones, I notice more: a vast pool of water, right at the bottom of the pit, shimmers in the darkness. A big machine sits abandoned halfway up a kind of track way on the far side of the pit. There's a little copse of bushes near a lean-to with a raggy tarpaulin stretched over it.

I clutch at Kos; I swear something moved between the bushes. As I watch, dark shapes seem to pour out of the ground and come running towards us.

The dogs!

I step behind Kos as the dogs fly up to him, licking his hands and jumping up. Kos bats them away, saying gentle things in another language.

"Is this where you keep them?" I ask.

Kos nods and smiles and reaches into his bag and shares out sausages and lumps of meat to his dogs. I avert my eyes from the drool and the sloppy mouths.

Kos reaches for me and I'm thinking this is NO time for a snog, but instead he unwinds Mother's scarf from round my neck. He mimes rubbing it in his armpit, then hands it back to me.

"You want me to rub my scarf in my armpit?"

Kos nods. "Dogs, Lexi. . ." He struggles to think of the next word. "Friend," he says eventually. I think I know what he intends to do. I turn away. I shove the scarf under my jumper and rub it in my armpit. Then I hand it back, feeling rather unsettled. Kos sniffs it and for a minute I think I might run away. How gross is this! But Kos is handing me back the scarf.

"More," he says.

I suppose I ought to be pleased I'm not smelly enough for him. I rub the scarf under my other arm and hand it back.

Monster dog appears behind us and I cringe away, but Kos puts a hand on my shoulder.

"Dogs hurt you last time because you wear wrong clothes," he says. "Not Lexi's smell."

What does he mean "wrong clothes"? I've never heard of being attacked because you're wearing the wrong outfit.

"You wear bad man's coat," he says. "Dogs know smell. Dogs think you are man."

Then it clicks. When I came up here with Owen that first time to look for Tyson, I was wearing Owen's jacket as mine had got wet.

"They attacked me because I was wearing Owen's coat?"

"Yes," says Kos. "They know his smell."

I wait for more information. But Kos says nothing.

"What is it with you and Owen? Is there something going on that I should know?"

"He hate me," says Kos. "Dogs look after me."

I'm trying to compute all this. I know Owen was pretty annoyed when Kos broke into our house, but isn't all this a bit extreme? And anyway, I was attacked *before* the break-in. So Kos and Owen must have some other history.

"Come on, Kos, tell me what all this is about."

But Kos just pulls a face which I am beginning to recognize. It means he's pretending he doesn't understand me and therefore doesn't have to answer my questions.

"So if you and Owen are deadly enemies, why are you showing me round?" I ask. "He's going to be my stepdad in a week's time."

Kos picks up a stone and flings it into the pool, making it bounce off the surface before it vanishes with a plop.

"Lexi hates him, too," says Kos, smiling at me. He taps his ear, indicating I should listen. Then he throws back his head and emits a long, high-pitched howl which grows around me and echoes off the quarry walls. When he's stopped, he puts his head on one side and listens. Within seconds, a couple of his dogs are howling back.

"There you go again, talking to the animals," I say. "I wish you would talk more to me."

Kos leads me to the fire and finds me a log to sit on. He chucks some twigs on the fire and I'm watching the flames spring up when something cold and wet presses into my hand, making me jump about half a mile off my log. It's the collie. He looks up at me with big yellow eyes. I wonder why all the dogs don't just run home? It must be their wolf genes stopping them, or maybe the fact that they all seem so busy and well-cared-for. Kos said he'd only taken dogs who were shut up all day. Maybe they're actually happier out here.

"Bolbi," says Kos, rubbing the dog's ears as it leans into him, slavering and panting with pleasure.

"Hello, Bolbi; please don't eat me," I say, shifting ever so slightly away. The fire is very nice but I'd rather have a nice clean radiator. You don't have to mess about with wood and matches and you don't get smoke in your eyes when the wind changes direction. Kos leans forward to poke the fire and a lock of dark hair falls over his forehead. I reach over and smooth the hair back. Look at me, I'm as bad as bloody Bolbi; I can't keep my paws off him. I sit back on my log and pretend to be deeply interested in the contents of my bag. Kos doesn't smell like the kids at school with b.o., but of a mixture of wood smoke and earth and sweat. He does need that bath, though. His hands are black with grime. In the firelight I see his fingernails are broken and packed hard with dirt. He is the filthiest individual I've ever seen. Why I am experiencing an urge to kiss him is beyond me – or maybe it's because nobody else wants to cuddle me these days. I bet he hasn't brushed his teeth for years. Mind you, I'm not looking so squeaky clean myself. There are twigs stuck in my hair, mud on my shoes, and the hems of my jeans are wet. Frankly, I'm a mess, and I don't like it, but Kos doesn't seem to mind how I look. He's looking at me like he wants to eat me. Maybe he does want to eat me.

"Who are you, Kos?" I whisper.

"Kos," he says, intent on discovering what I bring out of my bag.

"You only want me for my groceries," I say, handing him a bun and a bottle of beer. He demolishes these and looks up for more. I pass him another bun and open a bottle for myself. For an instant I have an image of myself feeding a tiny baby bird; a bird with a wide-open mouth. Kos's face develops a beak. I blink away the image and concentrate on Kos's long legs and dark features. *Lexi*, I tell myself sternly. *You do not fancy this man. He is a thieving tramp.* But he's lush-looking and he saved my life! It's not like I'm intending to marry him. I'm sixteen and it's good to have some fun.

When he's finished the bun, I ignore the good Lexi, the one who's whispering *no* in my head and I lean over and give Kos a kiss on the mouth, no messing. His mouth is hard and at first he pulls away a bit. I think I've startled him. He tastes of bun and smoke. It's like he's never kissed properly before. He suddenly seems like a shy little boy. I pull away, disappointed. I didn't feel anything. Never mind, I tell myself; practice makes perfect. Kos looks at me under his lashes. It's too dark to tell for sure, but I'd swear he's blushing. He won't meet my eyes. I hope I haven't blown it. Maybe he doesn't like me after all. So I'm caught by surprise as he leans over and kisses me back.

This time it is much more satisfactory.

*

"I don't know anything about you," I say, disentangling myself from him after a few minutes of snogging. I hate to admit it, but he's really very whiffy. It puts me off my stride.

"You smell," I say. "You need a bath."

Kos grins. "OK," he says. He jumps up, kicks off his shoes, and runs towards the pool, and before I know it he's splashing around in the black water.

"Lexi," he calls, his voice echoing over my head. "Come swim, you smell bad."

"I do not," I say, outraged. I walk over to watch him splashing around. It's really not so dark, now my eyes have got used it. I can see everything quite well, there's just no colour. I put a fingertip in the water. It's freezing.

"Lexi, come. . ."

"Maybe next time," I say, drying my finger on my jeans.

But then Kos wades up to me and is pulling me in. Cold water seeps into my shoes. "No, Kos," I shout in alarm, but Kos keeps tugging. Fear slices through me. I don't know this man very well at all. And he has a personal vendetta against Owen. And he's just shown me his secret hiding place.

"Lexi, swim," says Kos. And I shriek as the cold water reaches my knees.

Kos lets go of me and stands back laughing. It's all right, I tell myself. He is not going to do me in.

"Take that." I scoop up a handful of water and fling it into his face. This is a bad move because he retaliates and I am showered with cold quarry water. The dogs start barking in excitement and splash around the edge. There's Tyson, leaping through the water like a kid at the seaside. Maybe he is better off out here with Kos, than at home.

I focus on getting Kos as wet as possible, and we end up sitting on our backsides in the shallows and laughing.

A little later we're huddled by the fire. Kos has produced a big old blanket which I've got draped around my shoulders. My top half is a bit damp and my trousers and shoes are soaked.

"So tell me, Kos. . ."

But he flings his arm around me and goes in for another kiss. Oh dear, what have I started? I'm not worried. I have ways of keeping men at bay. But I have to say his technique is improving by the minute. Actually he has a very steep learning curve.

"Steady on," I say, wriggling away. "We're only snogging."

Kos springs up and bounds off. I watch the flames, hoping he hasn't left me to be eaten alive by his hell-hounds. But then he's back. I watch as he sets up a little spit arrangement and then takes out a knife. He watches my face, then turns his back to me. He starts sawing at something in the stones. The air is filled with the stench of blood as Kos skewers something dead and wet on his spit.

"Oh God," I say, edging my log back. "Is that another rabbit?" I can't watch this. I used to own a rabbit called

Benjamin. He allegedly died of natural causes when I was six, though in my darker moments I wonder if Devlin had a hand in it.

"Food," says Kos, grinning.

I put my head in my hands. What am I doing? I shouldn't have kissed him. I don't know what came over me. I wish I hadn't but when I get the urge to do something I find it hard not to carry it through. Especially with Kos. He's tall and broad, with muscles in all the right places. He's even got a bit of a beard for God's sake. I never ever thought I could kiss a man with a beard. I must be going mad. Maybe I'm getting carbon monoxide poisoning from Mother's house and it is affecting my brain.

I'm finding it hard to watch the fire now. It's lost its magic now there's a dead animal singeing and sizzling over it.

"Kos," I ask. "How long have you been here?"

Kos clicks his tongue and shrugs. He pokes at his rabbit. "Mother," he says. I wait, but if I'm expecting a revelation, I don't get one. "Mother, bird." He points to the sky and waggles his elbows.

"I think we can quite safely agree she isn't," I say a little crossly.

But Kos looks hurt. "Bird," he repeats.

I sigh. I really don't think this relationship is going to work out. But he's too goddamned handsome for me to resist. It's not my fault; I'm ruled by my teenage hormones.

"Well, my mother is a cow," I say just for fun. "A very clean one. And my dad, well." I pause to consider. "He's a sneaky rat. He lives in drains and turns up in places where he shouldn't. My brother. . ." I pause and think of low creatures. "He's a skunk, who quite rightly, spends most of his time locked away. And my stepdad." I shudder when I think of his face. "He's a gorilla, and he spends most of his time on aeroplanes and in pubs."

Kos nods as if he understands every word I say. Maybe he does! "Lexi?" he asks.

I quite like this. It's almost a conversation.

"Oh, I'm a swan," I say. "I'm bad-tempered, cocky and vain."

"Kos?" he asks shyly.

I smile. "You're a fox." And I lean over and kiss him on the mouth.

When the rabbit is cooked, Kos offers me some, but there's no way I'm eating it.

"Your need is greater than mine," I say in a martyred voice. I watch as he piles into the hot flesh. I notice again how thin he is.

"Look, Kos," I say. "Why don't you come home with me. You're not well. I'm sure you could get fixed up with a place to stay. If you're really desperate, you could stay with my brother in Bexton. He's a handful, though. He'll probably beat you up a bit until he gets used to you."

But Kos looks horrified. "Lexi shhh," he says over his rabbit.

168

"But. . ."

"Lexi SHHH," he says in a loud voice. I've upset him. He springs to his feet and I think he is going to run away.

"Chill," I say. "It was only a suggestion."

"Polis," he says. "Polis . . . hurt." He looks at me wide-eyed. "Police hurt Kos. Hurt mother."

I stare at him. "Who are you, Kos?" I ask softly.

"Kos," he repeats.

"Kos," I say. "Why are you here? Where's your mother?"

Kos licks his fingers. He looks at me for a long time.

"Bird," he says finally. "Far away."

This is too frustrating.

"What are you telling me, Kos?" I ask again. He makes a funny face, sucking in his cheeks and frowning hard. He starts humming. I'm about to ask him what he's playing at, but then I realize he's trying to stop himself crying.

"Kos," I touch his arm. "Is your mother dead?"

"Yes," he says. "Dead. Bad, bad men."

I don't know how long I stare at him; it feels like I'm in a dream. "Should we go to the police about this?" I ask gently.

His face clouds over. "NO POLIS," he shouts, pushing me so hard that I fall on my bum in the grass.

"Chill, Kos . . . I'm not too keen on them myself."

It looks like I've got yet another boyfriend who is allergic to coppers.

*

I'm creeping in through the back door at five o'clock in the morning. It's still dark outside. I'm tired and damp and my mind is racing. I know Kos could tell me more if he wanted. Sometimes it's like he understands every word I say, and he replies in good English, but if I move on to touchy subjects, like his mother or his family or where he's from, he starts grunting and giving me one-word answers and regresses to caveman mode. I keep thinking about what he said about the police and his family and I'm jumping to all sorts of conclusions. But it's hard to know what to think when I don't know all the facts.

It might be that he's talking about the police from his own country, wherever that is. It might be that he's from a family of thieves (like me!) and that's why he's got this fear. Or it might be something else. Something connected to Owen and possibly Beacon House Hospital itself.

I am beginning to form an idea where Kos might have come from.

I take off my coat, stuff my dirty shoes in a plastic bag and pour myself a glass of water. On my way upstairs I look up and get a jolt as I clock Owen watching me from the landing. He's all dressed up in his security guard uniform. Damn! He must have an early shift.

"Where've you been?" he asks.

"To get a snack," I say, pushing past him.

"But you're dressed," he says.

"I fell asleep in my clothes," I say, running up the stairs before he has the chance to say anything else. I go straight to my room and shut the door. I listen as he comes up the stairs and over the landing. I hear him breathing outside my door and I tense.

"*I thought you didn't like sausages,*" he whispers very low and soft. "*Especially mine. Did you have a nice midnight feast in the woods?*"

My heart misses a beat and I have to steady myself against the wall. I wait for ages, unable to move because I don't know if he's still there, but eventually I hear the front door slam and his car start up outside. He's gone.

Jumble

The first thing I thought when I finally woke up, round midday, was, *Dad's in prison*. It made me feel sick. I managed to mostly forget about him when I was with Kos last night. Maybe that's why I went up to Beacon Wood in the first place: to forget. But now it's all crowding in. I'm so pissed off that Dad didn't tell me the truth. On the other hand I would have given him an earful if he had. Mother thinks he'll be up for parole at Christmas, which would mean me staying here in Bewlea for another four months. This brings me on to the subject of Owen. He was so creepy last night, it was like a bad dream. But I don't see how he can know what I'm up to.

Downstairs Devlin is flicking through the TV channels. He's going home to Bexton today because he's scared someone is going to grass him up over breaking his ASBO. He's eighteen so it's OK for him to be living alone. But with Dad in the nick, there's no money at home to pay bills or buy food. If I go back with Devlin I'd have to get a full-time job and wave goodbye to college. And living with Devlin, without Dad to keep him in line, is like living with a lunatic.

And what about Kos? I don't want to abandon him.

I slip downstairs and steal Devlin's new white hoody from the kitchen and tiptoe out the back door without anyone noticing. I'm not going to say goodbye to Devlin. I'm still mad at him for mugging Ella, and I'm staying out of Owen's way because I don't want him asking any questions about last night. There's a jumble sale in the church hall this afternoon and I thought I might see if I can pick up something for Kos. He badly needs some new clothes. If I had loads of money I'd go to Bexton High Street and get him a complete brand-new wardrobe. I fantasize about kitting him out with some wicked new trainers, some cool, baggy skater-boy jeans and a couple of decent tops. Maybe this is weird of me. Am I treating him like some kind of big man-dolly? I push the thought from my head. There's nothing wrong with wanting your nearly-boyfriend to look good.

Half an hour later, I'm rummaging through old men's underpants with half the village. Ella's here, fighting over a blue woollen coat with Mrs Harris from the post office. Look at me! I never, ever thought I'd come to a jumble sale. See what living with my mother is doing to me! However, I've found a pair of jeans which I think will fit Kos, and also two tops and a thick sheepskin coat, all for three quid. Then I very quietly pay 20p for a pink sparkly top which looks as if it will fit me. Thank God Moz can't see me now!

I'm just handing over 60p for a pair of quite decent men's trainers when I am tapped on the shoulder.

173

"Why are you buying men's clothes, Lexi Juby?" It's Ella, and she's got two huge bags spilling over with dresses and shoes.

"They're for my mystery lover," I say, winking at the old bag who's manning the table and giving me a frosty look. Through the window I see the bus for Bexton pull up. I gasp as Devlin climbs on in broad daylight. He's so cocky. If someone recognizes him, he's in for it. I edge round the table to spy on him, earning myself another dirty look from the old bag. I think she expects me to make a swipe for her tin of 20p's. Devlin slouches down the central aisle of the bus, knocking into the seats. He arranges himself along the back seat, feet up and trailing his arm into the seat in front. He's such a psycho. Why did I have to end up with him as a brother? He twists round and looks right at me, so I duck. I cannot let it get out that I, Lexi Juby, have been seen in a jumble sale. Also, he's bound to have sussed by now that I've swiped his new hoody.

"Can I help you?" asks the old bag.

"I dropped a contact lens," I say, from the floor. "Don't mind me."

I hear the roar of the bus engine as it pulls away. I wait another minute and then get up.

Outside, it's a nice day. The sun is shining. Before I go to work, I want to see what Kos looks like in his new hoody. And now I am allegedly dog-proof, I don't need to worry about being savaged to death.

*

174

I lean the bike against the fence surrounding Beacon House Hospital and duck through the hole. I pick my way through the thistles and dying grass, treading carefully over potholes and bits of fallen masonry. For a moment I see myself, as if I am looking down from the sky. I see a small, grey figure, alone amongst the sprawling decaying buildings. Emily told me they sent mad women here a hundred years ago, and right now I'm picturing women in long dresses walking round the gardens in twos. The lawns are mowed and all the thistles have been pulled out. The statue has regained her nose and the weeds have gone from her dress. The clock tower chimes every half-hour. There's a crunch on the gravel path as a horse and carriage pull up by the main steps. A shrouded figure is led into the dark building. I give a little shiver. I'm glad I didn't live in those days.

I watch a robin land on the statue. What was she called? Lady Fallondale? Emily said she was buried under the padded cells. I shudder; it wouldn't surprise me if they still existed somewhere. But where is Kos? So far, I've only had to show up and he has appeared as if by magic.

Then I see him. He's walking on top of the wall which divides the hospital garden. I look again. Oh my God! It's not Kos, it's Jak! He's the last person I expected to see up here. I'm about to call out to him, but change my mind. If Kos sees us together, he might think I've given him away. Besides, I don't want to have

175

to explain what I'm doing up here to anyone. But what is Jak doing up here? I step behind the statue and watch him. Jak jumps from the wall. He takes off his glasses and puts them in his pocket. I must say he looks better without them. I wait till he has gone through the garden door before I move out from behind the statue. I hope the dogs don't get him. I don't want to have to do any rescue missions. I work myself backwards out of the garden, keeping watch in case Jak reappears. No wonder Kos isn't around. He must have seen Jak. I don't think I'm going to be able to give him his clothes today.

I pelt back through the garden to the fence. Ella's bike is leaned up against the main gates. This must be how Jak got up here, unless Ella is rampaging around the forest as well (which I sincerely doubt). I feel uneasy about Jak being here. He looked, I don't know, sneaky, like a spy. Of course it might be innocent, he might be just out for a stroll, but I think there's stuff going on that I don't know about. Or maybe he came up here to find me? He must have seen my bike, parked near his; maybe he's looking for some romance. I so hope not.

I'm cycling down the lane when I see something that nearly makes me fall off. Owen's van is parked by the side of the road. Owen is not inside it. I zip past, shuddering and wondering what this means.

I cycle home fast to avoid being overtaken by either Owen or Jak. I have a bad feeling about all this.

*

It's quiet at home. I collapse on the sofa. The sun has come out again and the front room is full of golden light. There's a nice, relaxed atmosphere now Devlin has left. He's the sort of person who makes everyone feel on edge when he's around. It would be a bad idea for me to go home to Bexton and live with him, though I do miss my old life. We'd kill each other, and from what Devlin's been saying, he fills the house up every night with his mates. I dread to think what they get up to. This is Devlin we're talking about, and he's not one to do things in moderation. That's it, I've made up my mind to stay here. I'm definitely better off out of it until Dad gets released and straightens things out.

I'm hungry, so I decide to brave the kitchen and hunt for some food. Mother is in there, doing wedding things. She hardly notices me these days, she's so wrapped up in the wedding. But as I'm frowning at the empty cupboards she goes and freaks me out by showing me a photograph of her intended flower bouquet and asking my opinion.

"I'm worried they look, oh, I don't know, too much of a cliché," she says. "I don't know if lilies and roses give the right impression. They're not really ME."

"It's lovely," I say without bothering to look at it properly. I'm ravenous and couldn't care less what flowers she's going to carry as she throws her life away on a big, disgusting troll-man. "I wish there was FOOD in this house," I snap, slamming the cupboard.

"And I wish you were nicer to me," says Mother.

I look at her in surprise. She's got new lines around her mouth and her face is looking pinched. I'd say she's lost five pounds too much weight. "You're always picking fault with me," she continues. "You never smile at me or ask me how I am. You act like you can't stand the sight of me."

"You never have anything good to say to me," I say. Owen's out so he's not going to come bounding downstairs to join in. All the same, I should walk away before I say something I regret. Mother picks up the empty net from a bag of oranges from the kitchen counter and fiddles with it, rolling it between finger and thumb.

"You're so angry, Lexi," she says. "Always."

I swallow hard.

"And you seem to go out of your way to annoy me," she says quietly.

I can feel the anger burning up in me. *Keep a lid on it, Lexi*, I tell myself. *Don't lose it. Don't lose it.*

"I'm your mother," she says. "I wish you'd show me some respect."

That's it. There's a little voice in my head telling me to keep my mouth shut. But I can't. Let's just have this out once and for all. "Why should I show you respect?" I say, turning on her. "You left me when I was two years old. What kind of a mother does that to her children?"

I can't believe I just said that. The words came from nowhere. I can't believe they left my mouth. They hang in the air between us. After a long silence, Mother speaks. She looks very small and even older than before and she won't leave that damned orange netting alone. I want to rip it out of her hands.

"The kind of mother who tried to do what was best for her children," says Mother quietly. She shuts her eyes. Ha! She ducked out of eye contact first! Ding dong. Round one to Lexi.

"I didn't leave for my benefit," says Mother. I snort in a teenage kind of way. I want to walk out of the room but I can't. I'm tied here. This is the conversation I've been waiting to have all my life. I'm excited and terrified.

"I know Dad's no angel," I say. "But why couldn't you have stuck around until I at least could do up my shoelaces?"

"I didn't leave because of your father," says Mother. "I left because of you."

I stand dead still. That's maybe a bit too honest for my liking – talk about opening a can of worms, this is a can of vipers.

"I wasn't a good mother," she says. "You were a stubborn child and Devlin was out of control."

I can't argue with any of those points so I wait for more.

"When you were tiny, neither of you slept properly. I'd be up for hours, night after night. And the tiredness ate away at me. I'd scream at you two for no reason. Sometimes I wanted to run away."

She doesn't sound like Mother any more. She's speaking in a quiet, sad voice I've never heard.

"One evening, when I'd finally got you both to sleep after an awful day, I opened the fridge and there was no milk. Your dad was away and I knew there'd be tantrums the next morning. I found myself leaving the house, locking the door and walking to the shop. It was only a few minutes away. I thought, *What if there's a fire?* But I knew there wouldn't be a fire. I told myself you wouldn't come to any harm, and I was back in fifteen minutes. I went upstairs to check on you and you were both sleeping peacefully. Safe. I told myself I'd never do it again. But I did, a week later. Your dad was away a lot then, working." She gives me a sideways look. "I ended up going out and meeting friends, going for drinks or to the cinema. Everyone thought I had a babysitter, and as soon as you were asleep, I'd be gone."

"But that's awful." I say. "Anything could have happened to us."

"I know," says Mother. "But I couldn't afford a babysitter, and once I'd had a taste of freedom I couldn't stop myself. I became happier, looking after you both in the daytime, knowing I could escape in the evening, even though I felt guilty. I started putting you to bed earlier and earlier. All day I'd be planning about what I was going to do when you and Devlin were in bed. I came home once," she says, "and you were crying out for me. You were standing up in your cot in your pyjamas. Your face was puffy with crying and covered in snot and tears, all the bed coverings were on the floor and you were freezing. You must have been awake for hours. It was one o'clock in the morning. That shook me up," she says. "I'd always told myself it didn't matter, because you didn't know. But now you did. I told myself I wouldn't do it again. But I did; I went out and left you the very next night."

I stare at my mother. I don't know what to think. I've never heard her talk so much.

"I didn't like being a mother to young children," says Mother, in her new, quiet voice. "I was no good at it. I didn't like the mess and noise. I thought it would never end. Your dad wasn't much help and I was exhausted all the time." She gives me a weak smile. "I much prefer you now."

I raise my eyebrows at this.

"Your dad wanted more children," she says. "I didn't. It didn't help our relationship."

"You shouldn't have had any," I say.

Mother winces.

"Eventually my friends got suspicious. Celia came round one day to have it out with me. She said she knew I'd been leaving you. She said people had been talking about contacting social services. She asked me what I thought I was doing. And I broke down and told her I couldn't cope. She said I should get help but I wasn't interested. I knew I couldn't be a mother."

Imagine fat Celia knowing all this.

"Soon after, during breakfast, I'd had a fight with Devlin, and then you fell off your chair and wouldn't stop screaming even though there was nothing wrong with you, so I walked out of the house, locked the door, put the key under the flowerpot, got in the car and drove. I ended up out on the motorway and I knew I wasn't going to come back." Mother wipes her eyes. "I left you both alone for thirty minutes before I pulled into a service station and phoned Celia and told her to go round to look after you. I left a message for your dad. Then I got back in the car and drove as far away from all of you as I could." Mother looks at me. There are tears pouring down her face. I have never, ever seen her cry before. I didn't know she could.

"Celia told me later that she found you sitting on the stairs, cuddling Devlin." Her voice breaks. "I'm sorry, Lexi. I loved you, but I couldn't look after you."

I'm silent. I'd always assumed she'd left us for a man. "Now you're older, I like having you round," says Mother, dabbing her eyes with a tissue. "I love the fact you're so independent. You're nearly an adult now. I can talk to you. I don't have to wipe your nose or be up half the night with you. You know I can't function without sleep. But it wasn't you and Devlin's fault; I wouldn't have been able to cope with any child."

There's a long silence. Very long. Using every ounce of restraint, I bite back all the evil things I could say. "So I'm unlikely to get a baby sister now you're marrying

Owen, then," I say eventually. Mother glares at me; then her face relaxes. She smiles.

"No," she says.

I walk over and take the orange netting from her hands. It's all knotted and frayed where she's been worrying it. Then I hand her a tissue. "I'd better check out this bouquet of yours," I say, picking up the photograph. "We can't have you going down the aisle carrying a cliché."

Hen

I'm on my way home from work. In the kitchens everyone was talking about The Wedding and some of the older female staff are going on the hen weekend (leaving for Cornwall tonight). But I was distracted because the first thing I noticed when I walked into work was a new poster stuck up in the bar.

£250 REWARD FOR INFORMATION ABOUT A VAGRANT, POSSIBLY CONNECTED WITH SPATE OF RECENT BURGLARIES, POSSIBLY LIVING IN VICINITY OF BEACON HOUSE HOSPITAL ESTATE AND FOREST. REPLY PO BOX 386

I was pretty freaked out by it, and even more so when Wendy told me Owen had put it up. Owen! I have to get to the bottom of what's going on between Kos and Owen. I'd ask Owen straight out, but I don't want to admit I know Kos. I'm going to have to be more careful. And now I think Jak was in the woods yesterday because he was after the reward money, not because he was after trying his lady luck with me. I shouldn't feel annoyed with him, as he probably thinks he's doing the community a favour. But I can't imagine how Kos would cope if he got arrested. I'll have to warn him about this. I'm glad Jak wasn't at work today; I don't think I'd have been able to act naturally.

At home, Mother is rushing around, preparing food and packing and panicking. The hens are having a meal here tonight before the minibus comes to take them to Cornwall. I always thought it was a bad idea but a couple of her friends can't go to Cornwall and Mother wanted to include them somehow. Everyone is supposed to bring something for the meal so Mother doesn't have to cook, but she's still going mad heating up canapés, emptying peanuts and crisps into glass bowls and skewering pineapple and cheese on sticks. I take over with the food and tell Mother to go and have a bath. She looks at me like she can't believe her luck.

"Go on," I say. "You shouldn't be doing this on your hen night."

We're a bit shy round each other after yesterday. I'm still getting my head round everything she told me. She as good as admitted she was the world's worst mother, but I don't hate her for it. I'm glad she was honest with me. Come to think of it, I don't know if I'd be much use with little kids either, all that bum wiping and spooning baked beans, but I can't see myself abandoning them either.

Earlier, Mother asked me again if I wanted to go

to Cornwall, but I said no. I'm not ready for this kind of thing with her yet. I need time to think about everything. So I said I had to work but I'd join the meal at pudding time to say hello, and I offered to wash up afterwards. See, I'm not all bad. It's also Owen's stag night. They're going drinking in the hotel. Mother has given Owen strict instructions that under no circumstances are they to come here. So I'll have the place to myself.

I pay a quick visit to Emily whilst all Mother's mates are arriving. I wanted more information out of her about working in Beacon House Hospital when it was a detention centre, but she's right into her scrapbooking at the moment and won't talk about anything else. I have to sit through three collections of Pregnant Celebrity cuttings before I can escape. When I get home, the hens are all still cackling over their first course, which is pasta willies with tomato and green beans. A lot of obscene jokes are thrown around. I stand in the doorway of the dining room. There are eight women and all of them are pissed. I recognize Lydia from next door and Celia, and a couple of receptionists from the hotel who I don't know very well. Even Mother has a rosy glow.

"There's my beautiful daughter," she slurs, and everyone turns to look at me.

I wish she'd say things like that when she's sober.

"Join us," says Celia, pouring me a glass of wine.

"In a minute," I mumble and flee upstairs. I remove

my dirty clothes and have a long hot shower, ignoring the banging on the door from Mother's pissed mates. The hot water pounds into the back of my neck. When I'm clean and changed, I go downstairs to assess the situation. They're finally on to the pudding, and when I slip in next to Celia, she gives me a nod. I watch as Mother eats – eats! – a whole plate of profiteroles. She must be absolutely hammered. That's easily 1,000 calories. I feel pretty shy, which isn't like me, but it's because they all know each other so well, and they've been drinking for a few hours now. Also, if they're Mother's mates, they'll be aware how we don't get on. Likely enough Mother has poisoned their minds against me and now they all hate me. I sit here, playing with my pink paper napkin amidst all the laughter and chatter, and wonder what Dad is doing. I picture him sitting in his cell, doing nothing. It must be driving him mad. What would he make of all this? Years ago, there must have been another hen night, only that time, Mother was about to marry him. Weird. I can't imagine them being in the same room, let alone being married.

The minibus turns up before they've finished their coffee. There's a scramble as everyone rushes around going to the loo, finding their coats and bags and apologizing to me for leaving a mess.

"I don't mind, enjoy yourselves," I tell them. "I turn to Mother. "Have fun. Make the most of your freedom."

"Come with us, babe," says Celia, giving me a hug. I

look at Mother and she nods and smiles. She really is drunk.

"I can't," I say. Is it my imagination or does Mother look disappointed?

"Come on," says Celia. "Bury the hatchet."

"Yes," shouts Lydia. "You're her daughter, for Christ's sake, you should be there." I bite my lip. This is what I was worried about. I like to think I'm pretty tough and can handle just about any situation, but a gaggle of drunken women wanting to force a cheesy reconciliation is too much, even for me.

"Girls," says Mother warningly.

"Lex-ie, Lex-ie. . ." a football chant starts up. This is awful. I feel cornered and got at.

"I'm sorry," I say. "You'll manage without me."

"Maybe she's jealous," slurs Lydia. "She wants Owen for herself." She's shouted down by the others but it's too late. I'm livid.

"I can't stand him!" I howl. "He's repulsive. I'd rather marry a monkey."

There's a silence. Mother opens and shuts her mouth. I do likewise.

"Have a good time," I say eventually. "I'm going to bed." Mother looks like she is going to say something but then Wendy runs in, late from work, with a bottle of bubbly. The cork explodes out the bottle and floats down under a small pink parachute and everybody laughs and gets their glasses refilled. The minibus driver comes in and starts ferrying baggage outside. A few minutes later,

I'm alone. I stare at the ransacked table for a long time. Should I have gone? Have I blown it for good this time?

After I've loaded the dishwasher and cleaned the kitchen I power up the computer in the sitting room. I don't usually use it because it involves sitting on the office chair which has Owen's bum imprinted in it. I hate fitting my bum into this. It's too intimate. Also the keyboard is all grubby where Owen's horrible fingers have been typing. Mother never goes on the computer. I'd tried to persuade her to do all her shopping online but she'd said, "Where's the fun in that?"

I place a cushion on the chair and type "Beacon House Hospital detention centre" into the search engine. I get offered a list of choices:

RIOTS AT BEACON HOUSE HOSPITAL

BEACON HOSPITAL CLOSES

BEACON HOUSE HOSPITAL UNDER INVESTIGATION FOR ALLEGATIONS OF RASCISM AND CRUELTY

FIRE CLOSES PART OF DETENTION CENTRE AT BEACON HOUSE

MISSING REFUGEES FROM BEACON HOUSE

I choose the first one on the list.

WEB NEWS

The manager of the beleaguered Beacon Asylum Detention Centre, Mr Timothy Holden of Safe Security (SS), said work was under way to ascertain how many, if any, detainees are still on the run after a riot which erupted after a disturbance between staff members and a group of female detainees last night.

Rioting detainees last night ransacked a communal eating area and started a fire in the a d m i n i s t r a t i o n wing, destroying thousands of pounds' worth of equipment. Also, computers containing information about the detainees were smashed in the confusion.

There is speculation that some women may have escaped. The centre also holds detainees' children.

Bingo. I read more. I learn that there was an investigation into the riot which was never made public. However, soon after, the centre was closed down, and Beacon House Hospital was left to rot. I also find some reports of cruelty there, long before the riot.

There was a little foreign kid in reception class at primary school everyone said was a refugee. I remember having to deliver a message to the infants' class; I was maybe ten, and this little boy, Idrin, had the teacher and classroom assistant peering into his mouth. I remember leaning over to have a look and being shocked at the row of grey teeth. I didn't think little kids could get rotten teeth. This boy was dead cute, though, and everyone said his family were refugees from the war in the Balkans. I took no further interest in him, or any war happening thousands of miles away. I was ten. I had things to do. But now I'm pretty sure Kos is also a refugee, like Idrin. It nearly all stacks up. But I have to find the connection between Kos and Owen. I know Owen worked up at the hospital as a security guard, but that's all. Maybe he was involved in the riot. Maybe he was responsible for Kos going missing. I just don't know. The website said the riot happened three years ago. Could Kos have been living rough for that long? Why hasn't he gone crazy? I think of his stolen dogs. Why hasn't he gone *more* crazy?

I click on another heading.

BODY FOUND IN DERELICT DETENTION CENTRE

WEB NEWS

Police have disclosed that the remains of an unknown female have been found, in a shallow grave, in the grounds of a former detention centre, Beacon House Hospital, in Bewlea, SW. It is speculated that these remains could have been there between one to two years. DNA analysis reveal no match with any persons missing in the era. Local speculation that the remains are associated with the period when the house. was a detention centre for asylum seekers have been dismissed by the Home Office as "scare-mongering and ludicrous". The derelict building is associated in the wider community with occasional vagrancy.

So who was she? It crosses my mind that this woman might be connected to Kos, but the dates don't add up. The riot was three years ago, some time before this woman died. She must have been a tramp or something, who knows. I give a shiver. How I hate that place.

I'm in bed, sleeping deeply, when I'm awoken by the door slamming. I look at my clock, expecting it to be deep into the night, but it's only midnight. What's Mother doing home this early? I sit bolt upright.

There are men shouting in the kitchen.

Stag

I'm wide awake and my heart is thudding. There must be at least ten of them downstairs. There's all this shouting and loud bursts of laughter and cheering. I lie still, listening to the crashing and banging and swearing downstairs. Something smashes and pieces of china spin over the floor. Deafening music erupts from Owen's speakers. The neighbours are going to go insane.

It's not Mother.

Why has the stag party come here? Mother banned them! Owen swore he wouldn't come near the place. And why do they have to shout at each other? My door looks thin and useless. I wish I had a lock. I don't like being alone in a house with a load of pissed-up blokes. I don't feel safe in bed so I get up and pull on my jeans and a jumper over my nightie. I slip on my trainers over my bare feet. Then I sit in the window seat and try to think. Calm down, I tell myself. Calm down. I'm being an idiot. What am I thinking? But I just get nervous around groups of pissed-up men and there's nothing illogical about that. I sit for ages, hugging my knees and listening to the commotion. There's a drinking competition, accompanied by lots of laughing. Then there's an argument (I can't make out what it's about) and everyone is shouting and a dog starts barking. It must be Toad. A couple of people leave after that, slamming the door. When they've gone, everyone left starts laughing again. I move back from the window when they pour out into the back garden, leaving the music blaring in the empty sitting room.

Six men are left. Owen, the Neasdon triplets and two others I don't recognize. And from the look of them, they're all absolutely hammered. Owen isn't looking so hot. He's wearing a parking cone on his head and one of Mother's camisoles is stretched over his fat chest; his man boobs flop around grotesquely. I crouch low and peer over the sill. It wouldn't do to be seen at this point. The men lurch around, crushing flowers, knocking things over and one of them takes a leak on the grass. Someone, I think it's Lucas Neasden, trips Owen over and starts yanking off his trousers. They're all drunk so I shouldn't really be feeling quite so shocked. The others go to help, and after a few savage minutes, Owen is naked apart from the camisole. He's pretty annoyed by now. The men take hold of an arm or a leg each and start swinging Owen. I ought to be enjoying seeing him humiliated, but I'm not. It's like I'm watching a pack of animals; they're out of control. It doesn't make me feel very safe. I wonder if I should creep downstairs and belt off to Emily's for the night. But I don't want to run into any of these men.

I watch the men swing Owen higher and higher. He's bellowing for them to put him down. Men are so weird. These are people who are supposed to be his friends. Then they swing him really hard and let go and he flies over the fence, his white, hairy body gleaming in the moonlight. Everyone shouts and cheers and claps. No one goes to see if he's all right. A box of beer materializes and they all sit on the grass and crack it open. They all start talking shit, but at least they're fairly calm now. A fat, hairy leg straddles the fence and the cheering starts again as Owen falls down into the garden, crashing into the flower bed. Someone throws his trousers at him and they wrap round his head. It takes him ages to put them on again because he keeps wobbling over.

A couple more blokes leave after that.

"Great night," they say.

It's not my idea of a great night.

I wish they'd all go home and take Owen with them. Things are calming down. Most of the stags have left. Everyone left is lying on the grass, drinking and laughing. I think it's just Owen and the triplets now. I'm just thinking about the possibility of going back to bed when Owen looks up at my window. I duck, but it's too late. We made eye contact, and I didn't like the look on his face at all.

The kitchen door slams. I freeze, looking round the room for some kind of inspiration. I think this is zero hour.

"Lexi," croons a voice up the stairs. "Oh Lexi."

It's Owen. He's very, very drunk. I can still hear laughter outside so I guess he's on his own. I really am in a situation here, but can't think what to do. I swallow. I'm scared.

"Lexi – shit." There's a loud bang. I think he's tripped on the stairs. I eye up my window. No good. I can't jump out; I'd break my leg and I wouldn't be able to run away. I spy my mobile on my desk and punch in Mother's number. I'm listening to the dialling tone as I hear Owen stomp upstairs.

In the garden there is a fresh burst of roaring laughter. They're all so pissed, they probably haven't noticed that Owen has gone.

And Mother isn't answering her phone.

Please leave a message after the beep.

Owen crashes into my room.

"Get OUT!" I scream.

"Can I have a cuddle, Lexi?" he says, lurching in the doorway. He's holding a half-empty bottle of absinthe.

"No," I say. "You're pissed, Owen. Get out."

"But it's my last night of freedom," he whines, edging closer. "Come on, Lexi, I know you like me." His trousers are wet and the camisole is ripping under his arms. His eyes are bleary with drink.

"I hate you," I say. "Fuck off and die." I like to make things clear. But I'm scared. He's big and he's drunk. His face is grey with red blotches and his mouth drools.

"Just a little kiss," he says and lunges for me, but I dart sideways and he misses. "Tease," he says.

"Go AWAY!" I scream. "Someone come and help!" One of those scumbags downstairs has to hear me, but the music is so loud and they're laughing at full volume. I can't get to the window because Owen is blocking my way. Oh Jesus. It looks like I'm going to have to employ The Last Resort. It will hurt him. A lot. And Mother will never forgive me. They wouldn't be able to have much of a wedding night, if you know what I mean.

Owen's getting cross now. He's calling me all sorts of vile names, and stepping closer. It's almost comical, me leaping away as he stumbles forward. But I know how strong he is. I'm going to have to be very quick.

"Sexy Lexi," he says and grabs my shoulder in a move that's surprisingly quick for a pissed old git. Here goes, then . . . first I need to twist, then. . .

"Oh-wen," says a voice from the doorway. "Whaa, wha . . . wha you doing?" It's Johnny Neasdon. He's so wasted it's hard for him to speak. I try to evaluate whether he is good or bad news. He wobbles into the room, puts his big paws on Owen's shoulders, and pulls him away from me, but Owen pushes him off.

"She's Paul-lah's little girl," says Johnny, frowning and blinking. "Whatcha doing?"

"Same as you'd like to do," says Owen. "You can't deny it." He spins me round and kisses me. His breath is foul and rank, like rotting eggs mixed with boiled beer and farts. "You're not as beautiful as your mother," he says. "But I'd still like a cuddle."

Footsteps pound up the stairs and Lucas and Matty appear in my doorway.

"GET HIM OUT!" I yell, twisting away from Owen. There's a belt of laughter as the brothers combine to pull Owen backwards, dragging him out of the room.

"She won't have me because she loves the rabbit boy," slurs Owen as he is marched downstairs. Lucas and Matty seem to find the whole thing very funny. I don't. I'm shaking. Johnny is hanging around in the doorway. He's so big, the top of his head looks like it's brushing against the door frame. "You OK?" he hiccups, trying to look concerned. He goes to rub his face, misses, loses his balance and nearly falls over.

"Bugger off," I say.

"Of course," says Johnny. He turns round but somehow trips and ends up sprawled on the floor. "I'll be gone in a minute. . ." he says. I breathe slowly and deeply. That was bad.

Downstairs the music is switched off and there's more laughing. Or is it shouting? I listen hard, working out what to do next. I can't think clearly. I'm too scared. I hear a gentle snore coming from the carpet. Johnny's out cold.

"*Come on, let's do it!*"

"*Now or never.*"

"*Do it, do it, do it.*"

"*Let's have us a stag hunt. Let's catch a rabbit.*"

They're working themselves up into a frenzy down

there and Toad is going mental, barking at them all. I sit deadly still, listening and waiting to see what they do next. If I thought I could sneak out undetected, I would, but I don't want to risk running into any of them. I'm stranded up here.

Now they're all chanting together.

"Stag hunt, stag hunt, stag hunt."

I think of Mother. I bet she and her mates are dancing away in some club. Yet again I wonder why she is really marrying this man.

"Run rabbit, run rabbit, run, run, run." Owen is singing at the top of his voice. *"Here come the brothers with their big gun, gun."*

I hear the click and squeak of the gun cupboard being unlocked.

Rabbit Boy

"Gonna catch us a big bunny," slurs a loud voice from the garden. "Gonna string him up on the gibbet. Got a new secret weapon." I rush over to the window. Owen's just below, standing in the flower bed peering up at me. He's got a large sack in one hand and a rifle in the other.

"Bye, Lexi bunting, Stepdaddy's going hunting, going to get a rabbit skin, to wrap a little Lexi in." He coughs and belches. As I stare, he raises his gun and I fall to the floor, banging my knee on the window sill. But Owen laughs and crashes out of the garden. I peep over the window sill, rubbing my knee, then crane my neck to look round to the front of the house. They're getting into Lucas's van. I can't believe they're going to drive; they are all well over the limit. Actually, I can believe it; they're all so plastered they think they can do anything. But the main thing is, they're leaving. I hear shouting and swearing and a bang as Owen chucks his sack in the back. Doors slam and the van judders forward, then stalls. They start it up again and I watch the tail lights zoom off into the distance. I don't want to be here when they come back.

There's a groan from the floor and I jump, but it's only Johnny. He sits up and rubs his head. He looks blearily around the room, like he can't work out where he is. Then his gaze lands on me.

"Hello," he says. "Have I missed the party?"

"They've all left," I say. "Only you to go. Do you need help on the stairs?"

"How did this happen to me?" Johnny fingers his eyes. I don't bother to answer.

"Thanks for sorting out Owen," I say quietly. If it wasn't for Johnny – well, let's not go there.

But Johnny looks embarrassed. "Don't mention it." He heaves himself up, finds it a bit too much and leans heavily into the wall. "I'll always help you, Lexi. I think you're a . . . a . . . very nice girl." He's trying really hard to act sober. "Am I in your bedroom?" he asks, looking alarmed.

"You're just leaving," I respond.

"I'm so sorry, Lexi," he slurs as he tries to get up. "I'll be off now." But he's so wobbly he falls over. Again. I look at his massive body, twitching on the floor. I don't think Mother is going to believe me about all this. She knows I hate Owen's guts. She'll probably think I'm trying to frame him in order to split them up. Johnny moans and sits up, his head in his hands.

"If you're going to hurl, please don't," I say. "Mother's just had this room redecorated."

"Sorry," repeats Johnny, and he drags himself out of my room, bouncing off the walls on his way. I hear the bathroom door slam and the delightful sounds of him voiding his stomach contents into the toilet. Nice. Whilst he's busy, I stuff some clothes in a bag and go downstairs to survey the damage. The kitchen isn't trashed by, say, Devlin's standards, but there's enough devastation to make Mother mad. There's bottles, empty glasses and fag ends everywhere. The glass in the back door is cracked and some joker has unwound an entire bog roll. The floor is covered in footprints, soil and food wrappings. The fridge door is wide open and a milk puddles out of a smashed bottle. I open the door into the living room, take one look at the formerly white living-room carpet and quickly shut it again. It gives me some satisfaction to think what Mother will say to her husband-to-be about all of this. Then I have to sit down because my legs have gone all wobbly. I suppose it's because of Owen's attack.

Johnny stumbles into the kitchen, wiping his mouth. His eyes are sunk into his head and he has a trail of vomit on his shirt. He looks ten years older. However, the puke seems to have done him some good because he is now able to stand upright without falling over. "I'm really sorry, Lexi," he says, and sounds like he means it. He looks round at the mess. "Where did everyone go?" He's speaking more clearly now.

"You're lucky you passed out," I say. "Owen and your brothers have just buggered off in a van, with a rifle. They're all hammered and I'm fairly sure they're all going to get arrested very soon."

"Where were they going?" he asks, seeming more alert.

I tell him that they said that they were going to go rabbit hunting. I suppose it's some kind of sick party game drunk men get up to. Johnny goes pale. Assuming he's going to be sick again, I pass him the washing-up bowl. "But I'd rather you threw up outside," I say. "Or even better, not at all."

Johnny shakes his head; he's not going to be sick. He asks me to repeat who was in the van.

"Owen, of course, and your brothers," I say. "They've been gone for half an hour. Why, do you want to join them? I shouldn't if I were you. It's only a matter of time before they get pulled over." I'm hoping Owen will get done for possessing a firearm whilst drunk driving and he'll get nicked. The wedding will have to be cancelled and all will be well.

"I've got to stop them," says Johnny. He wobbles forward, then lurches into the wall.

"Doesn't look like you'll get far," I say brightly. "Shall I call you a cab?"

"Lexi, I'm so drunk, I'm useless," mumbles Johnny.

I decide not to hang around. Johnny seems OK, but after my experiences tonight I'm not taking any chances. I'm getting out of here. I pick up my bag and edge round him to get to the door.

"Let yourself out," I chirp, opening the front door.

"Lexi. . ."

I slam the door. Then I take a deep breath and head

off for Emily's house. I hope she doesn't mind me getting her up in the middle of the night but I'm too scared to stay at home. Also, Owen will never find me there. I run through the quiet streets, glancing at the houses with the curtains pulled tightly shut. I think of all the normal people inside, sleeping and dreaming. I worry that Emily won't let me in. Who answers the door at two o'clock in the morning? I'll just have to see. I get to number four Hope Street in ten minutes flat, and I'm out of breath and hot.

Emily's house is all in darkness. I am about to ring the bell when, freakily, the door opens.

"Lexi, is that you?" Emily puts her head round the door.

"Yes," I say. I don't know how she does it. She must have a sixth sense.

"Come in, come in." Emily is wearing a pink padded dressing gown over a full-length flowery nightie. Her long hair lies in a grey plait down her back. She shuts the door behind us and takes my hand. Her fingers are freezing. "It's Owen's stag do tonight, isn't it?" Emily peers at me. "I saw them in the hotel bar earlier."

"That's right," I say. "They've had too much to drink and Mother's in Cornwall. That's why I'm here."

Emily looks at my face. "Come and sit down, you look pale." She leads me out of the dimly lit hallway into her sitting room, where she has one small lamp switched on. I sit in the armchair by the window. Then Emily says something unexpected.

"Lexi, is Kos OK?"

"Y-y . . . yes. I mean no. I don't know what you mean." I stammer. I didn't think that anyone knew about him except me. And Owen.

"It's all right, I know you see him. Kos has told me about you," says Emily. "In his way," she adds.

"But how. . .?" I begin, but Emily grabs my hand again.

"You must promise not to tell anyone else I know him."

"But. . ."

"Promise me, Lexi."

Emily looks so worried that I agree to the promise. She lets go of my hand and sits back in her chair. "I expect Kos is in one of his hidey-holes. He's probably safe enough," she mutters.

"Emily," I snap. "Tell me what's been happening here."

She wipes her sleeve over her wrinkly old face, shudders and takes a deep breath. "His name is Kos," she says in a shaky but clear voice.

"Yes. . ." I say through clenched teeth.

"He was held at the old hospital, you know, when it was a prison for foreigners."

"Asylum seekers," I say.

"There was some trouble up there, and afterwards there were rumours flying round the village that there was a boy at large in the woods."

I knew it!

Emily continues. "Some of the guards – Owen and the Neasdon triplets – organized a search, but they didn't find him." She hesitates. "The centre was a big place; people were coming and going every day. It was all quite chaotic. Even I saw that and I was only the cook. I never knew how many I was going to need to cook for. And during the trouble – well, it was a riot – a fire destroyed the records, so no one really knew who was supposed to be there. I watched the buses when they took the inmates away, but I didn't see Kos or his mother. So I went up there, night after night, looking for him." She sighs. "And eventually, I found him. I hope I was always kind to him, and that's why he showed himself to me. He wouldn't have survived on his own, dear," she says. "So I brought him food. He was only a boy." I look at Emily and try to make sense of what she is telling me.

"But why didn't you contact the police?" I ask. "Surely Kos would have been better off if you'd taken him in?"

Emily snorts. "Lexi, Beacon House Hospital was the place they kept illegal immigrants, people whose request for asylum had failed. It was the last place they were taken before they were deported. And Kos came from a terrible place, full of war and murder. If I'd turned him in, I might have been sending him back to his death!" Her voice is shaky and I look away from her. There's a lot I don't know about the world. But something is niggling at me, something Emily has said.

"But what about his mother?" I ask. "You said you didn't see her get on the buses either."

"Did I?" says Emily. "I get so confused." She looks up at me and I watch her biting her lip. She's not confused; she's hiding something. "Kos came for food when you first visited me," says Emily, brightening up. "That was a scare!"

"The stray cat," I say, remembering how Emily seemed to be gone for ages and I discovered her bean mountain. That must be why she has all this food – for Kos. Emily gets up and walks over to the window; she twitches the curtain open, takes a quick look out, then pulls them together again. "I wasn't there," she says, turning to me. "I wasn't there to see what really happened. But I do know that ever since the riot, Owen and the Neasdon triplets have tried to find him."

"They've gone off with a gun," I say slowly. "They said they were going to catch rabbits. They've taken Lucas's dog."

"Oh . . . oh, Lexi." Emily looks over at me. "Then we have to warn him. Kos stole that dog last spring. But it came back after only a few days. Lexi, those men nearly caught Kos just before you arrived here last month. They used the dog to hunt him; it knew his smell, you see, and it knew where to find him. They cornered him in the superintendent's old lodge. But Kos got away by the skin of his teeth. Lexi, you have to go and make sure he's all right."

I move the curtain back and look out of the window.

The street is empty, quiet, normal. It's hard to believe that all this is happening.

"But why?" I say. "Why are they behaving like this?"

Emily twists her rings round and round, one after the other.

"Owen has a very good reason for wanting to catch Kos," she says quietly. "Lexi, there's things I haven't told you." Her voice falters. "Things I can't tell you. But I do know that boy is in danger."

"Emily, you have to tell me," I say sternly. "If you're going to make me go up there, you have to tell me everything you know."

But Emily just shuts her mouth and gazes at me. Tears dribble out of the corner of her old eyes.

"I can't, Lexi," she whispers.

I have this sinking feeling in the pit of my stomach. I really do not want to go up there alone, with that lot rampaging around.

"Come with me," I plead.

Emily shakes her head. "I'm too old. I haven't been able to get up there for ages now. I used to walk up there but now I need my third leg." She points to her stick, leaning against the wall. "That's why he's been breaking into people's houses. I can't feed him any more. I can't even get to the shops very easily." She looks at me. "I don't drive, dear," she says, just to make it clear.

"Can't we just call the police?" I plead.

"No, Lexi, I told you before, Kos is an illegal

imigrant. And he's a criminal. If the police get wind of him, he'll be finished."

I try to think what to do. Then I remember Johnny Neasdon.

"I'll always help you, Lexi."

Mad-Bird

*J*ohnny's lying snoring on the sofa. I eye him for a minute or two wondering if I'm doing the right thing, then nudge his shoulder with my foot.

"Wake up," I say. "We've got to stop your brothers." Johnny opens his eyes and looks at me. He smiles, then shuts his eyes again. "JOHNNY," I shout. "I need the keys to your van. If you don't give them to me, I'm calling the police, now!" He opens his eyes then.

"Owen said you were fiery," he says, sitting up and rubbing his head.

"Johnny, it's three o'clock in the morning. Your brothers and Owen have gone off to the woods with guns."

Johnny swings his big legs off the sofa and groans. "You know him, don't you?" he says, blowing sick-smelling breath into my face. "Owen says you go up and meet him. He says he's seen you steal food for him."

"Who?" I ask, though I'm pretty sure I know who he's talking about.

"The boy," says Johnny. "The boy." He rubs his hands over his face. "The bloody rabbit boy." I stay quiet, watching him. "He's been after him for years." Johnny makes an attempt to get off the sofa but slumps back.

I stare at him. "Why?"

Johnny finally gets to his feet and looks down at me, long and hard. "Lexi, you don't want to get yourself mixed up in all this."

"I already am," I say. "What's happened? Why's Owen got it in for him? Tell me."

"We have to stop them," he says. "But I'm over the limit, I can't drive up there."

"I'll drive," I say, and Johnny looks at me in surprise. Devlin taught me to drive years ago.

I'm about to get into a car with a drunk man I don't know very well. I must be insane. I ought to phone someone, tell them what I'm up to. But I can't get hold of Mother; she's not picking her phone. Ella is away for the weekend, and Dad obviously isn't available. Moz is still in Cornwall and Devlin always makes things worse. I don't know what I'd say anyway; Kos would go bananas if I told anyone about him, even though it seems half of Bewlea knows all about him anyway.

"*Stay quiet of me,*" he'd said. "*Promise.*"

Johnny's car is parked in the next street. I have to stop him falling in the gutter a few times. He won't stop apologizing. It's quite irritating.

"Ouch." Johnny smacks his head on the door frame as he's getting in the passenger seat. I look at him and decide to text Ella and Mother, just in case I don't make it back.

Gone wiv J. Neasdon 2 Beacon Wd 2 stp Owen shootin some 1.

The inside of Johnny's car is unexpectedly clean and tidy. It smells new. I hope this means it's going to be easy to drive. I spy a torch in the side of the door and slip it into my jacket when Johnny isn't looking. I breathe in and adjust my mirrors so I can see behind; then I move the seat forward so I can reach the foot pedals. I turn the ignition key and the engine fires up. I reverse the car out of the driveway. As we join the main road, I hope I'm not going to be the one pulled over by the cops.

"You smell nice," hiccups Johnny. "Like flowers."

"You smell disgusting," I mutter. "Like puke."

Johnny faces me. I glance over and see he's looking worried. "Sorry, I didn't mean anything dodgy," he says. "You're young enough to be my daughter."

"Good," I say. We drive past the green. There's nobody about. "Come on, then," I say to the man slumped in the seat next to me. "What's all this about? What's rabbit boy?"

"Lexi, I can't tell you this stuff. It all happened so long ago." Johnny sighs.

"No," I interrupt. "This is happening right now. Tell me why Owen and your brothers have gone off into the woods with a shotgun, in the middle of the night." I choose my words carefully. I don't want to admit I know Kos, even though Johnny seems to know I do. "I heard all about the riot. . ." I say, prompting him.

"You have?" Johnny sounds surprised.

"I know Owen was involved," I say. I don't know if this is true but Johnny seems to be swallowing it.

"Owen was like our fourth brother. Lots of stuff happened up there, it was that sort of place, but we always stuck together. We were a team."

"What sort of stuff?" I ask, fumbling around for the indicator as we turn out of the village. I soften my voice. "You can tell me, Johnny."

He scratches his head and hiccups. "Lexi, I've never told anyone about this before." I wait for him to continue. Johnny gives a sigh; then he starts talking.

"It was Christmas, we had a party. Everyone had way too much to drink, you know? The weather was bad. Days of rain. We really let our hair down."

"You had a party in the prison?"

"For the screws. We thought we deserved it. It was a tough job." Johnny looks at me appealingly. "The place itself was always dark and depressing and some of the women inmates were pretty mad."

"I really feel for you," I say.

"There was this one woman, she was attractive but she was also a troublemaker. Everyone called her Mad-Bird. The week before the riot, she'd got half the women on a hunger strike. And she would never do as she was told. I know a lot of the staff thought she should be taught a lesson."

213

A shudder runs through me.

"This isn't the sort of thing you should be hearing." Johnny leans forward and cradles his head in his hands. "You're so young," he mutters.

"Yes it is," I say grimly. I change into fourth gear and we zoom down the empty road.

"Mad-Bird started something, I think she'd been winding up somebody; anyway she started screaming and things went a bit crazy," says Johnny. "The other women piled in to help her and the guards panicked. Some bright spark decided to try to separate the women from their children, you know, to try to make them calm down. But it didn't work. It made things worse, much worse. There was shouting and screaming and people chucking things. Somebody started a fire. There weren't enough staff to control the situation. Nobody knew what to do. It was bedlam. The kitchen staff were so scared they barricaded themselves into the kitchens and the managers locked themselves in their offices." Johnny's words tumble out in a torrent; now he's started talking, it's like he can't stop. "A couple of our mates hid out on the roof. People were just vanishing. Everyone was scared. There were only a few screws left, trying to keep charge. It all went a bit mad and violent, you know?"

"No," I say.

Johnny sighs. "Mad-Bird had a bad time with fire in her home country. She smelled the smoke and freaked and managed to get past the guards and out into the grounds. She had her little boy with her. She got over the fence, God knows how. Someone went after her, but she was gone."

Johnny sits back in his seat and closes his eyes.

"What happened next, Johnny?" I ask softly.

"I can't tell you," says Johnny. "I'm sorry, Lexi. I'm drunk. I shouldn't have said anything at all. It's just that you're so easy to talk to. And it's been hard, keeping this to myself all these years. It wasn't right, what happened then."

"What happened to the woman and her boy?" I ask. But I think I already know the answer. Johnny gives me a long, searching look.

"Lexi, it's best not to dig all this up. Really."

"You have to tell me," I say. "You can't hide these things for ever."

"No, I can't tell you," says Johnny. "Lexi. . ."

"It was Owen, wasn't it?" I say. "He was the guard who followed the boy and his mother out into the woods. But he didn't bring them back with him. They escaped, or at least the boy did. And tonight Owen's gone to look for him. gone to look for him. *But what happened to his mother?*"

"She could be very violent, Mad-Bird," says Johnny. "I swear she wasn't right in the head."

"But where is she now?" I ask. "And why is Owen hunting her son like this?"

"Just drive," says Johnny.

Torchlight

As we hurtle through the dark roads, my mind is racing. I'm thinking that Owen did something very bad the night of the riot. I'm thinking murder. The idea makes me go hot and cold. I'm thinking it was never found out, but that there was a witness.

Kos.

Kos was the little boy. And somehow he escaped, and Owen has been after him ever since. Does he know he's being hunted tonight? When we get there we'll, oh, I don't know what I'll do. I'll make it up as I go along.

"Lexi, sweetheart, when we get there you must stay in the car," says Johnny. "It's not safe for you. You don't know my brothers. . ."

"Fine," I say.

It seems to take ages to get to the turning for Beacon House Hospital. As we drive up, I peer out into the darkness and of course I can't see anything. I stop the car by the main gates. There seems to be little point in hiding. Owen's van is parked on the grass, a little way off. I can't tell for sure, but it looks empty.

"Lexi," says Johnny. "I'm so sorry. . ."

"Don't get yourself shot," I say, clicking open my seat belt and scrambling out of the car. I don't know for sure whose side he's on yet.

"Lexi, wait. . ."

I leave the door open and run out into the moonlight.

"Lexi. . ."

But I've soon left him behind.

The hospital, as ever, looks empty and dead. There are no lights in the windows and no noises. The moon is bright enough for me to see fairly well as I skirt round the building. I'm trying to be quiet but there's a crunch as I step on something plastic lying in the ground. After that, even my breathing seems too loud. I pause, thinking I heard voices coming from the wood. Yes, there are definitely voices, but they're a long way off. I can't make out what they're saying. If I was in a film I'd have some kind of radar screen with a heat-seeking sensor which would show Owen and the brothers in red dots moving in relation to me. But this isn't a film. This is real. And I have no technology beyond my sixteen-year-old brain.

I hope Kos is in his big room, all wrapped up in blankets next to the fire. Or even in his horrible smelly hut. I'll check there first. But as I pick my way towards it, the hut is all in darkness and I can't smell smoke. The door is slightly ajar, and as I step inside, I know straightaway that there's no one inside, even though I can't see a thing. I go back outside and look up at the hospital. I really, really do not wish to go back in there.

*

217

One month ago on Friday night I was at the cinema with the girls. It was my last night before I was sent away. After the film we snuck into the pub and got Moz to buy the drinks (she looks about twenty) and got chatted up by some students who were home for the weekend. We had a great night. I remember I was wearing my pink heels and my black dress. I remember getting annoyed because my shoes got a scuff on them. Now look at me! I'm standing in a massive forest, in old trainers, with jeans over my pyjamas and no make-up. Somehow I have to find a wild man and smuggle him away before he gets shot by my new stepdad.

Life is rich.

Come on, Lexi, I tell myself, *you've been in sticky situations before*. I walk towards the house. I don't want to switch the torch on because I don't want to draw attention to myself. I duck as a grey shape swoops over my head and flies off into the trees. I think it's an owl. I open a gate and pass through a doorway in a stone wall. I'm walking between two buildings, the main hospital and a separate building, which is long and squat. It's darker now; the moon has gone behind a cloud. Vast bushes grow everywhere. This is crazy. I'm never going to find Kos. But I know I can't just go home and wait either. My head is spinning with the information I have learned.

I come out of the bushes and walk over a paved area which isn't as overgrown as the rest. The moon comes back out from the clouds and I can see better. As

I'm stepping back down into long grass, something gleams in the moonlight, catching my eye. I step back so I can see better and decide to risk switching on my torch. A square of metal with serrated edges, attached to a kind of metal plate, is fixed to a chain in the ground. I back away rapidly. I think it's a trap and I nearly stepped in it. It looks strong enough to snap my leg off. It's a really horrible thing. I need to spring it before it hurts someone. How many more of them are out here? Did Owen put it there? I wouldn't put it past him. Maybe this was what he was carrying in his sack. I suppose I need to find a stick to set it off. But it's scary. The thing is massive. Assuming it works on the same principles as a mousetrap, I root around outside for a stick. I find a bit of plank and decide that will do. I set my torch on an alcove in the wall so that it's shining down on the trap, then, holding the end, I plunge the plank into the centre of the trap.

SNAP! The plank twists out of my hands as it's grabbed by the metal teeth. It breaks in two and falls to the ground. I'm jolted by the force of the spring. I ought to go home. Now. The place could be littered with these things. The thought is terrifying. I'll be no use to anyone with a broken leg. It'll be like walking through a minefield.

I look up at the stars. Kos is out here somewhere.

I head for the workshops, searching the ground for any more traps, but a gust of wind carries voices with it. Owen is getting closer. I snap off my torch. I'm beginning to feel like the hunted one now, never mind Kos. I creep round the side of the building. There's a window, with half the board torn away. I peer in, but it's too dark to see anything. The men's voices are getting louder; they're maybe five minutes away. I crouch behind a pile of lumber and stifle a squeak as a rat darts out over the grass. Owen and the Neasdons are just round the other side of the building. The men are whispering, but they're not managing to be very quiet.

"Look, Toady wants to go that way."

"Nah, it's cold tonight. He'll be in the hospital building."

"So we'll never find him."

They sound like they've sobered up a bit.

"*Run rabbit, run rabbit, run, run, run.*" That's Owen. "*Here comes the farmer with his gun, gun, gun. He won't get by without his rabbit pie, so run rabbit, run rabbit, run, run, run.*"

I peer through a gap in the pile as they walk into view. Owen is in front, followed by Lucas and Matty. I see Toad straining at his lead and I shrink back. I don't want him to smell me.

"Lexi could lead us to him." That's Lucas's voice. "Maybe we should have brought her with us."

"And then what? Don't be bloody stupid," snaps Owen. "I'm about to marry her mother." He stops and rummages in his bag, bringing out a large metal object. I think it's another trap. Where does he get all this stuff from?

"But how are we going to find him?" whines Matty.

"He could be anywhere. How do we know he's going to get himself caught in one of these things?"

I put my hand to my mouth in alarm.

"I've found some of his hiding places. I know the paths he takes, just like a little rabbit. He's not going to expect to step in one of these things. He's not going to be watching the ground. Besides, we got Toady."

I hold my breath. Oh God, Kos, where are you?

Owen holds the trap up. "I set two of these beauties yesterday. We've got to get him, tonight or very soon. Lexi knows him; it's only a matter of time before he tells her everything. And there's the boy who's been sniffing around."

There's a silence before Matty asks, "And what are we going to do once we've got him?"

I bite my lip.

"Are you serious?" asks Owen. "I've been hunting this little scut for three years. Look, Matty, I'm not going to hurt him badly. I just want to teach him a lesson and find out what he knows about Mad-Bird. That's all. I need to know what I'm dealing with. That's all I've ever wanted. I got the rest of my life to get on with and I'm sick of having this hanging over me. Did he see us do it, or didn't he?"

"I'm not getting involved in anything serious, Owen," says Matty. "Not this time."

"You're in it up to your neck already," says Owen. "And you know it. None of us wants this kid going to the police."

The men move off. I want to hear more, but I'm too scared to follow them. Besides, I've got to find Kos.

I wait a few minutes before creeping out from my hiding place. I edge round to the corner of the building and look round. Three shadowy shapes move off through the long grass. I follow, treading softly through the deep grass and listening to them murmuring to each other. This way, I might get to see where they've laid their traps. I can't believe my mother is intending to marry this man. I thought he was out here tonight because he was drunk and crazy, but it sounds like he's been planning it all along. They pause by the ruined statue. Then move on. They walk fast but clumsily; they're not yet fully sober. The beams from their torches play on the ground ahead. I can't get too close; they might turn and see me. I hope Kos is hiding out somewhere, far away. I even hope he's off on a burglary job. Anywhere but here. I hear the men talking again. They're going to check some of the traps in the forest. I ought to go with them, but a weak feeling has come over me. I can't bring myself to go back into that dark forest; the ground might be riddled with traps. I can't do it. I'm no use to Kos in the forest. I look up at the blank walls of the hospital. And I'm not going in there either.

I've made a decision. I'm going home and I'm going to call the police. This is all getting too scary for me. I'm out of my depth. I'm never going to find Kos. He's probably miles away. I'm the one in danger. Someone could be watching me now. . .

But then there's a noise on the very edge of my hearing.

The wind blows a chill over me; it crawls up my back, like when you get in a hot bath on a cold night. I hear it again. Someone, far away, is moaning. I try to think clearly but I'm scared. I hate this place. It stinks of evil, down to every last brick and window. I'm scared of the dogs, of Owen and Lucas, and I'm afraid of the mantraps. And most of all, I'm terrified about what might be making that noise. But I have to find out what is making it.

I walk in the direction I think the sound is coming from, between some outbuildings and out on to the wide, flat garden area. I walk close to the edge of the main building on a kind of concrete ledge which is grey in the moonlight. I move slowly, quietly. Every step I expect to hear the clang of metal and feel unbelievable pain as metal teeth close on my leg. I'm listening hard. I so hope I don't have to go in the building. I couldn't. Not in the darkness. It would kill me. I'd die of fright. I might fall in a basement again. The bulk of the hospital buildings stand between me and the forest so I don't know what Owen and his lot are doing. The wall curves round and then inclines to a level area. It might have once been another garden. There are greenhouses collapsing against the walls, and an old garden roller with a rotted handle lies half-buried in weeds. There's a doorway in the brick, with the door hanging off its hinges. I pass through to the other side. I'm following a kind of path where the grass has been flattened. I haven't heard the noise for a while. Maybe I was hearing things, or perhaps it was that owl. It wasn't Kos. He's bound to be safely hidden. He's not stupid. I could go home and phone the police, give them an anonymous tip-off that there's a gang of pissed-up blokes rampaging round the ruins with a gun. It's madness for me to stay out here on my own any longer. I look behind me at the forest. I see torchlight flickering on some far off treetops. I'm safe for now.

There it is again, a terrified whimper, an animal cry of pain. A human animal. And it's coming from inside the main hospital building.

"Oh Kos," I whisper. "What have they done to you?"

The Laundry

My stomach knots with tension as I get closer to the moaning. I'm walking through a gravelled yard which, like everything in this place, is riddled with weeds and piled up with rubbish. There's a small wooden side door standing wide open. I edge closer, following the noises. I feel small and young and vulnerable. What am I doing out here? I'll take the quickest look round the door, then I'll go home. Kos is probably safe somewhere, miles away. Maybe this noise is just one of his crazy dogs having a bad dream.

Something is moving around in there, groaning and panting. The noise echoes out into the yard. It's dark noises. Animal noises. My instincts are telling me to run away.

I slip in something. For a minute I worry I've stepped in something one of Kos's dogs has left behind. But there's a strong metallic kind of smell, not like dog poo. There are wet, dark stains on the stones beneath my feet. I shut my eyes.

I think I'm walking in blood.

I like to think I'm not a soppy, useless girl. I can drive a car, pick locks, win fights and run fast. And

225

unlike some of my friends, I know how to wire a plug or change a fuse. I can fix punctures, operate a TV remote and climb trees. I'd feel stupid if I couldn't do these things. I still love all the girly stuff, like clothes and gossip. I just like to be able to do things for myself. But there's one thing which really freaks me out. Blood. I'm just not good with it. I don't mind my own but anyone else's just makes my stomach feel weird and makes my head go all swimmy. I go cold and clammy. A few times Devlin has come back from a fight with a busted face, blood all in his ears and pouring out his nose. I can't stand it. And my ex, Chas, had a missing finger. It freaked me out. I couldn't look at it. I don't even like to think about blood. It's my fatal weakness. I'm not proud of it. Once Devlin had to have stitches in his chin, and Dad was on his phone in the waiting room, so I said I'd go in with him. I stood there, being Mrs Cheerful to Devlin, whilst all the time this horrible pressure was building up in my chest until I felt I couldn't breathe. I knew I had to leave the room and I stumbled out, leaving Devlin in the middle of his stitching, and I went and sat in the surgery car park with my head between my knees. I felt like a failure. There's something about blood. I can't even say the word without feeling funny. It's the stuff which keeps us alive. It's way too precious to spill, even a drop.

I could never be a nurse.

And now the familiar sick feeling is rising up in me. I don't even know for sure that this IS blood, but the fact that it COULD be is enough. I concentrate on breathing slowly and deeply.

Aaaahhhhh.

Someone nearby moans softly. Like they don't want to make a noise but they can't help it. I'm going in. I must be mad.

I walk up the steps into the hospital and step inside, scarcely daring to breathe.

A trickle of moonlight through the broken window illuminates the room. There's a large double sink on one wall and three narrow tables standing in a line. I touch one and draw back. It's made of porcelain and is icy cold. I switch on my torch and shine it round the room. Paint bubbles off the walls and fat, corroded metal pipes run out through the ceiling. There's a doorway in the far wall; the door itself is propped up against the wall. I examine the floor. It looks solid, but it slopes into the middle of the room, where a large grill covers a drain. I step into the room and read the remains of a typewritten notice, stuck to the wall.

NO EATING IN THE MORTUARY.

Eeek! I nearly drop my torch. I'm in the room where they laid out the dead. And I actually touched one of the tables. I don't like to think of the mad dead bodies which have been laid out here, years and years ago.

I hear the sound again, coming from deep in the building.

"Kos," I whisper. "Where are you?" The dark stains on the floor lead through the doorway. I grit my teeth and cross the room. I'm going to have to venture deeper into the hospital. I follow the trail, trying not to think too hard about what it might represent. I'm trying not to panic; I keep telling myself that the danger – i.e., Owen and his blood brothers – is outside. Therefore I am safer inside. And I need to help Kos. I could never live with myself if I abandoned him now. I have to go on, even though I swore to myself that I'd never set foot in here again. I shine my torch ahead of me. I'm in a low-roofed hallway. Even though the floor seems safe, I keep close to the walls and test the ground with each step before I put my full weight on it. The floor is littered with debris: broken glass, bits of wood, plaster from the ceiling, and rubbish. It smells of damp. At the end of the hallway is an open door. I get a wash of déjà vu. This has happened before; this feels like a memory, or a dream, or maybe a nightmare. I see myself, a small figure, picking through the debris, edging through the darkness towards something unspeakable. I step through the doorway. I hold my hands out in front of me because it is very, very dark in here. It's like my torch isn't making any impression on the darkness. I'm aware of the sensation of space around and above me, and I walk into a large, high-ceilinged room. There's a big arched window through which the moonlight streams. Broken tables are stacked up in one corner and there's a faint smell of smoke. I look around, unsure where to go next. This place looks like a dead end. But I hear moaning again, much closer this time but still muffled. I see a doorway I hadn't spotted before, and when I step over to it, I see a narrow flight of stairs going down. And there are dark splashes on each step. I really, really don't want to go down there. I don't want to leave this moonlit room. It feels relatively safe compared to what might be down there. My elbow knocks into a metal pole leaning against the wall and it falls, clanging on to the floor. The noise echoes round the room. Everything goes quiet. It feels like the whole house is holding it's breath, listening. I wait, the hairs on my body prickling. I'm breathing so softly I can't even hear myself. When I've got myself together, I shine the torch down the stairs. The treads look solid; I press my foot on the first one and it feels firm. I wonder if there is water down there, like at the other side of the house.

Very slowly, I start climbing down the stairs. I don't allow myself to think; I just keep moving. It's not a big flight of stairs, and I soon find myself in the first of a chain of cellars. This is a bit freaky because the brick arches are the same as the ones back in the front of the hospital, where I fell in the water. But now I'm standing on dry ground. I shine the torch beam round the walls, where rows and rows of large box-like machines are stacked up. There's also a big central table. I feel a breeze on my face and see one of the walls has partially caved in and the lawn above is growing into the room. I could probably get out that way, if need be. I walk into the next cellar – this one is stacked with old chairs and crates, broken buckets and piles of bricks. High up the wall there's a row of broken grilles through which I can see outside. A bundle of rags lies huddled in the far corner. Tentatively, I edge closer.

The bundle spasms, arms stretch out, fingers claw at the ground. His head jerks this way and that. He doesn't know I'm here.

"Kos!"

I run to him.

He moans. "Lexi, Lexi, help Kos." He's slumped up against the wall, wedged between two large washing machines. A puddle of blood pools out from under him. I bend and put my hand on his arm.

"It's OK, babe, I'll sort you out," I whisper. With a great effort, he tries to sit himself up, but it makes him pant with pain. He points to his leg and slumps back against the wall. "Lexi," he says, grabbing my arm so hard it hurts, his fingers digging right into my muscle. "Lexi." He stinks of blood and sweat. I force myself to glance in the direction of his leg. I breathe out slowly as I see vicious steel teeth biting into the flesh of his calf and his leg bending back at the wrong angle. I'm really not good with blood. Spots are appearing in front of my eyes. I can't believe what I'm seeing and I don't want to be part of the picture. Kos shudders and moans and pulls at the metal encasing him, but after only a few seconds he lets go.

Come on, Lexi, I tell myself. *This isn't about you.* I take a deep breath and my head clears a little. "What are

230

you doing, messing around down here? Are you trying to make me give you another kiss? Hey? Make me feel sorry for you?" I witter on, touching the metal and working out how I can free him. Then I feel his arms groping around me and we hold each other close, me kneeling in the dust beside him. He's so thin, it feels like I'm hugging a child.

Kos suddenly lets go of me, pushing me away, twisting round and moaning softly.

In the gloom I see a chain and a long stake covered in earth. Kos must have dug the peg out himself, God knows how. Then he must have dragged himself in here. I grit my teeth, switch on my torch and examine the trap. It is caught fast round his leg. I see torn flaps of skin and lots and lots of blood. I go to give Kos a kiss and change my mind. It's like he's not Kos any more. He's like an animal. I lift his tattered trousers to look at his leg but have to turn away. Through dark blood and shredded skin, I think I see bone gleaming. My stomach grinds and I feel light-headed. I touch the trap. It is cold and hard. I grab the jaws and try to pull them apart. They're stiff and rusty. I pull and strain so hard I worry that I'm going to burst the blood vessels in my eyeballs, but it doesn't budge. My fingernails rasp on the metal. Finally it gives a little, but then the blood under my fingers causes the metal to slip away and the teeth clamp shut again on Kos's damaged flesh. He screams, long and hard, and I blink back the tears.

"I'm sorry, it's all right, I'm sorry." I won't try that

again. I need to stop the bleeding. But how can I do that when the teeth are still biting into his leg? I don't know how to help him. I look helplessly at him. "Don't worry, I'll sort you out," I say brightly between clenched teeth. Though really I'm horrified. I'm worried that his leg is going to *come off* if he keeps struggling like that. I can't look at it, let alone try to treat it.

How do you comfort someone in this much pain? I take off my coat and wrap it round him. His breathing sounds awful, like a rasping old man. I get out my mobile, just in case, miraculously, there's a signal down here and I can call an ambulance, but there are no bars on the screen at all. We're on our own. I have to get the bloody thing off. I look around for something to help and see a broken-off broom handle leaning against the wall. I fetch it, then take off my hoody and my T-shirt, not looking at Kos, then put my hoody on again. I wad my T-shirt into a sausage. I dry my hands on my trousers, then gently grip the teeth of the trap.

"No, Lexi," groans Kos softly. But I'm going to do it. I have to. If I've found Kos, that means Owen can too. The metal budges again and I strain to hold it open; I pinch it open so hard my fingers cramp. I stuff my T-shirt sausage in the narrow gap between the trap and Kos's leg; this means, if it springs shut again, it will have to bite through three inches of material first. I don't let go. I grab the broom handle and gently feed it in. Kos helps me. He's focused on freeing himself, rather than the pain. Glancing sideways, I realize how he came to survive all these years out here on his own. He's pretty tough. I wedge in the broom handle and together we lever open the trap, slowly and painfully. There is a sudden clang, Kos groans, and for a second I think it has sprung shut on his leg again, but the jaws lie apart. We've done it. Kos gives a big sob as the bloodied evil thing slides off. It's odd what comes into your head, but I remember the game where you have a twisty wire with a current running through, and a metal lollipop loop, and you have to guide the loop over the wire without touching it and setting off the buzzer. Only in this case the loop is a jagged toothed trap, and the wire is flesh and blood.

Blood. There's lots of it.

"Kos," I whisper. "Everything's going to be fine." He's shaking and shivering and his teeth are clacking together. He clings to me, panting with pain, as I wrap the T-shirt round his leg to try and stop the bleeding. I wish I knew what to do but I got chucked out of Brownies before I got to my first aid badge. The leg needs washing and stitching and gallons of antiseptic, but I can't do any of that. Kos doesn't make a sound. He's in another place and isn't communicating with me any more. He's concentrating on breathing and staying alive. I'm worried about the fibres of the T-shirt getting stuck in his wound. But I haven't got any choice. I need to get him to hospital. I worry, just for an instant, that once he is in hospital, he will be picked up by the police and deported, back to God knows where. I look at his pale face. If I don't take him, he might die anyway. From the way his leg is bent, I think it might be broken. I look at the horrible, evil trap lying close to us. I jam the broom handle down on to the metal plate and it slams shut with incredible force, jerking the pole out of my hands and snapping it in two. I remember Emily. If I can get Kos to her house, we can work out what to do from there. I only hope Johnny is still up here with the car.

"Kos. . ." I begin, then stop. I hear men's muffled voices and snap off the torch. Kos hears the voices too, and his breathing quickens. How did they get so close so quickly? I look at Kos's white, terrified face. He can't move very far or very fast.

"Kos," I say. "We have to hide, you understand? Hide, hide."

"Polis?" he whispers.

"Yes," I say. "Come on."

He heaves himself up and leans heavily on me. But I don't know where to take him. The men sound like they're just outside, I can hear them through the gap in the wall.

"Look at that," bellows someone, probably Lucas. I hear Toad barking.

They must have seen the trap is missing.

"YES," Owen screams in delight. "Yes, yes, yes."

Kos trembles. "Go," he whispers, giving me a push. I hesitate. I could go, and run for help. . . But I'd be too late. The three men would find Kos.

They are almost upon us and Kos is breathing so hard that I worry that he's having some kind of attack. "Quickly," I say, "into the machine." I hold open the door of one of the massive washing machines and urge Kos to get inside. He hesitates. "Do it," I say. "It's our only chance." He drags himself in, giving small groans of pain, and I quickly squeeze myself in after him. Oh God, I don't know if this is the right thing to do.

"*Run rabbit, run rabbit, run, run, run.*"

It's Owen, singing softly. His voice echoes in from the passageway joining the mortuary to the laundry. He's nearly here.

"*Here comes the farmer with his gun, gun, gun.*"

"Shh." I hush Kos as he lets out a little whimper when I sit on his foot. My neck is all bent forward. We're hunched up and squashed together in this massive drum. Some kind of oil soaks into my trousers and a loose rubber seal, stiff with age, digs into my head.

"*He won't be fine, without his rabbit pie.*"

Through the round perforated door, I see two dark figures step into the room. I hold my breath and squeeze Kos's hand.

"*So run rabbit, run rabbit, run, run, run.*"

"Looks like we caught ourselves one big rabbit," says Lucas, toeing the trap. They're right next to us. If I wanted I could reach out and touch Lucas's back.

"Not a rabbit," says Owen, stepping close to our machine. "A dirty little rat. A rat I've been trying to catch for three years. Well, I've got you now, you little rodent. You scummy little thieving rat. I've got you now." He pulls open the machine door and a beam of light hits our faces.

Wolves

"Gotcha," says Owen, peering in. "Gotcha gotcha."

"Is it him?" asks Lucas, hovering behind.

"Hello, Owen," I say, blinking in the torchlight. "Do you think you could ring for an ambulance?" I try and sound like it's normal for me to be hiding in an ancient washing machine in the middle of the night in a derelict hospital.

"Christ." Owen steps back.

"No, it's Lexi." I ease myself out of the machine. "Your future stepdaughter." I make my voice sound bright and chirpy, but I'm terrified. "Hello, Lucas, where's Matty?" I wave at him. "I just got a lift up here with Johnny. He's up here somewhere." If I act like everything's normal, maybe it will become so.

Owen is silent. I think I've spoiled his moment.

Lucas clears his throat. "Owen, man, what's this?"

"Bugger off, Lexi," says Owen in a dangerous voice. "You know nothing about this. Go home and put your fingers in your ears."

"No," I say, trying not to give away how scared I am. "You're drunk, Owen; don't do anything stupid." In reply, Owen passes his torch to Lucas and raises his gun to his

237

shoulder. I hold my breath – he's never going to shoot *me*, is he?

"I don't think Mum is going to like it if you fire that thing," I say brightly, aware that I'm shielding Kos from the gun. How far am I going to have to go to save this boy? I don't want to get hurt; I don't want to be a dead hero. I could run out of the room and vanish into the woods. I could survive this.

I don't move.

"She'll never know," says Owen, but he doesn't fire, he just stares at me. I watch him, trying to work out how drunk he is.

"Get out of the way, Lexi. I've got unfinished business here."

"Owen, man," says Lucas. "You can't, not with her here."

"Then GET RID OF HER!" he roars, the gun wobbling on his shoulder.

"Hello, gorgeous," says Lucas. "Want to take a walk?" He grabs my shoulder and propels me into him.

"No," I gasp, twisting away. The cellar is filled with the smell of rotting meat. I hear scuffling, and Lucas lets out a shout as we are surrounded by a snarling river of teeth and claws, as dogs stream around us, growling and barking. Kos slides out of the drum and shouts something. Owen swears and the gun goes off. The noise is deafening and bounces off the walls. I can't help shutting my eyes. There's a thud and a yelp. I wait for a moment to see if anything hurts. Then open my eyes. I'm OK. I haven't been hit. I dive to the ground, dragging Kos with me. He groans in pain as we hit the deck. The air is full of yelping and snarling and growling and snapping, but for once, it isn't directed at me. Kos's dogs surround us. I think there's about six or seven of them, and the bigger ones are going for Owen and Lucas in a big way. I watch as my old friend, Monster, leaps up for Owen's throat, but he punches it away. Another dog growls and moans on the ground. He's been hit. It's a big bony animal, so thin his ribs are showing, and there are big clumps of soil stuck in hard balls to the back of his legs. I watch, horrified, as he drags himself out of the room.

"You shot Tyson," I shout to Owen, who is backing away from the rows of teeth and trying to get cartridges from his belt. The gun slips from his hands and drops to the floor.

"Shit," shouts Owen, kicking the big Alsatian as it goes for him. It falls but bounces right back and makes a leap for him. Owen smacks it over the head with his torch and the light goes out. The darkness is only broken by the faint moonlight coming through the grilles and from the hole in the wall in the next cellar.

"Come on, man," says Lucas. "There's too many. Shit." I think he's been bitten. I see a shadow run out of the cellar, with a smaller one running alongside, nipping and biting his shins. I hear Owen's voice.

"You're lucky this time, Rabbit Boy," he says. "But

your little girlfriend won't always be around to save you."

Dark shapes creep towards him, quivering and snarling.

"RAAAAHHHH!" roars Owen, and half of them shrink away. But then they creep back. There are too many dogs, even for him. They follow him out, jumping up and snapping. I hear swearing and yelps and crashing.

"I'll be back!" screams Owen from the stairs. "And I'll shoot all your bloody hounds."

Then he's gone.

On the floor, Kos is breathing hard. I guess he's lost a lot of blood. He needs urgent medical help but I'm too scared to leave him in case Owen comes back. And once he's in hospital, will I ever see him again? What will happen to him? I prop him up against the washing machine. The movement obviously hurts him, as he lets out a little yelp.

"Kos," I whisper. "What do I do?"

He makes a chuckling noise in his throat. Oh God, I hope it's not the beginning of a fit or anything.

"Kiss," he says. So I do. I give him the kiss of my life, through all the sweat and blood and stench. Then I draw back, my heart thudding, and notice a golden light streaming in through the grilles in the wall.

Dawn. At last.

"Come on," I say. "Let's get out of here before they come back." But I can hear crunching feet in the next cellar. Kos and I stare at each other. How can Owen be back so soon? Where are the dogs? He's going to finish us off, I know it.

A light appears in the doorway, followed by a dark shape. I can't see who it is.

"Leave him alone, you monster!" I scream. "He's done nothing to you." Kos moans in pain.

"It's me," says the figure. It's not Owen's voice. It must be one of the triplets. But there's something familiar about his shape. He shines the torch upwards into his face.

"Jak?"

"I heard noises, dogs. . ." It is Jak. It's hard to believe.

"What are you doing. . ." I begin. But he's not looking at me. Before I can stop him he's come across the room and is crouching beside Kos, talking gibberish to him. Kos looks totally confused.

"Back off," I order. "Or I'll kick you." I'm not having him handing Kos in for the reward money.

Jak stays put. So I kick him, hard. But as I'm doing so, I swear I hear him say, "Kos?"

"Oww, get off, Lexi, I'm not going to hurt him," howls Jak, rubbing his leg.

"Mercenary," I say. "Go and get help and don't even think about claiming the reward money."

"Lexi," says Jak; he can't take his eyes off Kos. "I think I've found my brother."

Sanctuary

Kos stares and stares at Jak. I look between the two. The dawn light reflects off their faces. Brothers? I'm shivering with adrenaline and cold. It's hard for me to imagine that Kos has relations of any kind. He's just Kos. Wild, crazy Kos. Wild men don't have brothers who work in hotel kitchens. There's a lot I don't know. But at the moment I don't care. I just want to get Kos out of here. Jak is squatting by Kos saying stuff I don't understand; he's saying the same thing over and over. *Vella, vella, Kostandin.* But Kos is shaking his head.

"Look," I say. "I don't know what you're up to. But we have to get Kos out of here. Owen will be back any minute."

"The dogs were chasing them into the forest," says Jak, unable to tear his eyes away from Kos. "We've got at least a few minutes." Kos shuts his eyes. This is too much for him. His head droops. We have to act fast. One of us is going to have to go and get an ambulance. Hopefully Johnny is still here. But if I send Jak off to get help, there's always the worry that Owen will get back here before the help does. I decide that, if it came down to it, Jak is bigger and stronger than me, so he stands a better chance of standing up to Owen.

"I've found you," says Jak.

"You'll lose him again in a minute if we don't do something," I say crossly. "Only this time it will be for ever."

Johnny is parked too far away for Kos. We need to find him a new hiding place, then go and get the van. We heave Kos to his feet and each wrap one of his arms round our necks and half-carry him out of the cellar. We climb the steps and stumble back through the mortuary. I get a huge sense of relief as we step outside into the dawn.

"The chapel's just over the way," I say. "Let's take him there." It's not a great hiding place but it's got to be better than going back into the main building. And now we've bound his leg, at least there won't be a trail of blood for Owen to follow. Kos comes round a bit now we're outside. He even hops to help us over the rougher ground. He isn't heavy, but he's holding himself stiffly, so he's awkward to move. His fingers claw into my shoulders and it bloody hurts. I can hear shouting and barking coming from deep in the woods.

We keep moving.

The chapel is a smallish building with a pointed spire and grey walls. We climb the crumbling steps to the main doors and lower Kos to the ground and try and work out how to enter. The door is padlocked shut. I examine it. I'm good at locks, but this one is corroded with rust and is beyond me.

"Stay here," says Jak, heading off round the back. Despite everything, I feel a tiny bit miffed. Who does he think he is, ordering me around?

I stroke Kos's hair. In places it has matted into dreadlocks. It's sticky with dirt and blood. Kos bends his neck to look at me and smiles. I look into his huge brown eyes.

"Is he your brother, Kos?" I whisper.

Kos shrugs. "Leg," he says. "Hurt." Fair enough. I don't know if I'd be bothering with a long-lost relative if my leg was mashed, either.

Jak reappears. "I've found a way in," he says. Round the side of the chapel is the remains of a small wooden door. The wood is coming away from the hinges. Jak gives it one hard boot and the whole lot crashes to the floor. The noise echoes out into the still morning and makes me nervous, but I can still hear the barking, some distance away in the forest. I think we're safe for now. We step inside the chapel. The floor, predictably, is covered in broken glass. It's gloomy in here, but it looks like someone has been inside at some point in the last five years and swept away the rubbish from the central aisle. It's a small chapel, with a vaulted ceiling and a few – mostly smashed – stained-glass windows. Maybe it's the growing light, but it's got a totally different atmosphere to the main hospital building; it feels calm and safe in here. Or maybe this is just wishful thinking.

We make a bed for Kos by sweeping the plaster and

dust from a pew, wedging in a couple of footstools alongside, and padding it with dusty old praying cushions. I put a cushion under Kos's bad leg and give him a kiss as he lies down. Then I make Jak give his jumper for a covering. Kos sighs and shuts his eyes. The T-shirt binding his leg is dark with blood.

"There's a van parked just down the road," I say. "I'll go and bring it nearer." Giving Kos one last pat, I run out of the door; then I stop, turn round and come in again.

Jak is bending over Kos, muttering nonsense to him.

"How do I know he's your brother?" I say. "What if you're in with Owen? What if you're going to hurt him when I'm gone?"

"Lexi, there's not time to tell you everything," says Jak in his Euro accent. "Only you should know that I came to this country eight months ago, as soon as I turned eighteen. I'm looking for my brother and my mother. They went missing five years ago from this place."

We stare at each other for a minute. I suppose they do look a bit alike. I have to make a decision now. Either to stay here and wait for whatever happens next, or to go out and get help.

"I was a prisoner here too," says Jak. "I was thirteen years old and got separated from my family in the riot. After it was over, I was deported. My grandmother survived the war and I've lived with her ever since. I swore I'd come back to find my family when I was old enough. I grew this –" he strokes his beard "– as a disguise. I didn't want anyone to recognize me." He takes off his glasses and hands them to me. "Look through, see, they're plain glass. I don't need them."

I look through the glasses. They don't magnify anything.

"They found a body up here a couple of years ago," says Jak quietly. "I think it was my mother. But I can't say anything yet, because I'm trying to track down her killer." He looks right at me. "I think I've nearly found him."

"If you're lying, you've had it," I say menacingly. "I'll bloody kill you."

It's times like these I realize I'm a Juby.

"Don't be so crazy, Lexi, just go," says Jak, wrapping his coat round Kos. "He's been lost for five years, Lexi. His family want him back."

"So if he gets deported he won't get murdered by the state?"

"No, Lexi," says Jak. "The war is over. We live in peace."

That will have to do. I run out into the morning. It's quite light now. A flock of tiny birds fly up in my face as I run, reminding me I need to be careful where I put my feet. There might be more traps. The grass is shining wet with dew and the leaves are falling from the trees. I crawl out under the fence and join the road. The van is still there, but Johnny isn't. And when I look through the window, I see the keys aren't in the ignition where I'd left them. Bloody Johnny has abandoned me! I can't believe it. I thought he liked me! I check my mobile again but there's still no signal. The forest surrounds me, still and dark, echoing with distant barking. I don't know whether to go and fetch help; I'd have to run to the main road and flag someone down, or go back to the chapel and make sure Kos is OK. I still don't know if I believe Jak. I decide to go back and see if he's OK. My imagination is racing, though, as I head back to the chapel. What if Owen does come back? He's got his gun. This place is so massive he could do in all three of us and hide us anywhere. He could chuck us back into the cellar. I grit my teeth and head back.

Back in the chapel, Kos has drifted off into a kind of sleep. At least I hope it's sleep and not a coma or something. Jak is cradling his head in his lap.

"Go and get help," I say. "Now. We can't use the van. You'll need to run to the nearest house. There's one on the main road. Call an ambulance and tell the police about Owen and his gun. That should get them here quickly."

"Lexi, I've been searching for my brother for five years," says Jak. "I'm not leaving him now."

Do I trust him? What if I get back and they've both disappeared? I'll never forgive myself. Just then Kos opens his eyes. He looks up, clocks Jak and thrashes out of his arms. "Lexi," he says. "Leg hurts."

I settle myself on the pew and put my arms round him. Jak looks hurt. "Give him time," I say softly.

Jak nods. He doesn't want to leave Kos but he knows he has to. He kisses him on the forehead and crunches out of the chapel.

Then everything is very quiet and still. Kos settles into my arms. I listen to his breathing and watch as he slips back into sleep. I look at the altar at the front of the chapel, and wonder if mad people used to get married to each other in here years ago. I think of all the funerals held here, and Sunday services with inmates twitching in the pews. It's hard to just sit and wait. I look round for a better hiding place. But thoughts of dark crypts and basements are not appealing.

We can't hide for ever.

I wish Dad was here. He wouldn't be afraid of Owen. He's been through some tricky times and he knows how to act in an emergency. But he's not going to rescue us. He's locked away in prison because he's a thief and liar.

No, I just have to sit tight and wait for help to arrive.

Somebody's here. I duck below the pew; Jak can't be back yet.

"Seeking sanctuary, eh?" My insides turn over. I peek round the edge of the pew. Owen stands in the doorway, in silhouette against the dawn sky. I can't believe it; only five minutes ago I heard shouting and barking in the woods. How can this be? Kos wakes at the sound of Owen's voice and looks at me, alert and afraid.

"Lexi, what am I going to do with you?" Owen speaks in a friendly, wheedling tone. "Come out and have a chat, I'm not going to hurt you." He doesn't sound drunk any more. Quietly I move the footstools and pull Kos to the floor. I urge him to crawl under the pew into the one in front. But as we are worming over the dusty floor I get a flicker of rage. I have a vision of Owen looming over us with his gun. I'm not going to take this lying down. I gesture for Kos to stay where he is and I step out into the aisle.

"I've had enough of you," I say bravely. "Harassing me all the time. Why don't you just bloody well leave me alone?" A column of light shines on the stone floor. The madness is over. It's morning. I'm not going to let him shoot us.

"Come on, Owen," I say. "You're not drunk any more." I stare into his grey, beer-mottled face and wonder if I'm doing the right thing. It may be morning, but for Owen it's still night-time.

"Go home, Lexi," he orders. "Now."

"It's over, Owen," I say.

"I couldn't agree more." My eyes open wide and I gasp as a woman walks into the chapel, wrinkling her nose in distaste at her surroundings.

"Paula . . . what the hell are you doing here?"

"I might ask the same of you." Mother steps down the aisle. She's wearing high heels! They click over the stone floor. She's wearing very tight black jeans and the pink rhinestone T-shirt and she is absolutely not afraid.

I don't think I've ever been so pleased to see anybody in my life. Mother! Johnny steps in behind her. She walks straight past Owen and comes up to me. She looks worried as she puts her arms round me.

"I didn't hear my phone. Are you all right?"

I nod, speechless, suddenly conscious of how wet and dirty I am, and how I'm dressed in my nightie and jeans and jumper. I must look like a crusty. Kos's blood has soaked my jeans and my hair is everywhere, like a mad old woman.

"I didn't think you two were due in church until next week," I say. I'm not afraid of Owen any more now she's here.

"Did you remember the ring?" I ask, turning to him. But he's gone.

Johnny stands in the doorway of the church holding out his hands as if to say, What could I do?

Mother looks down at me. Though she's looking a little tired, she's immaculately made up, as ever. "Johnny said I'd find you out here somewhere."

"Owen. . ." I begin.

"Don't worry about him now," interrupts Mother, looking at Kos. "We'd better take him to hospital." She looks at his leg, then at me. "Look at the state of you!"

"Mother, get a grip," I say crossly.

"Sorry," says Mother. "You're quite right."

Then everything's a blur of Kos getting over the grounds and between the buildings. Mother isn't much help carrying him, but we give her the job of checking the ground for traps. We're struggling along when Mother stops and exclaims.

"What's that?"

She runs over the grass, not easy in heels, and stoops to the ground. I can't imagine what can be causing this reaction. Then I see Tyson lying dead in the grass, his tongue lolling out of his mouth and his jaw frozen in a snarl.

"What happened?" asks Mother, her voice breaking.

I think the wedding might be off.

Sazanna

Mother's car is parked by the gates. The gate is locked, but as I'm working away at the padlock, Jak and Johnny tear away a section of the fence, making a gap big enough for us to help Kos through. Mother wants to go back to fetch Tyson but I persuade her that we'll come back for him, and that getting Kos to hospital is the priority. Mother climbs through the fence and runs ahead to her car. She smoothes a plastic bag over the front passenger seat.

"No point in ruining the upholstery," she mutters.

Kos allows himself to be loaded in the car, but he won't let go of my hand. Jak, Johnny and I squeeze in the back and Mother drives us away from Beacon House Hospital. My arm feels like it is going to fall off, but I don't let go of Kos. To my surprise, after only a few minutes his grip on my hand loosens and he falls asleep. Mother is acting like she drives injured wild boys to hospital every day of the week. Every now and then she'll say something like:

"Does anyone mind if I open the window? Your friend smells."

Or:

"I hope nobody moves Tyson before I get back."

I'm about to ask her what she is doing here at all when Jak opens his mouth and tells us his story. I keep trying to butt in to ask questions but he doesn't seem to hear me.

His family are Kosovo Albanians, and were frightened of the violence that Serbian forces and Albanians were unleashing upon each other during the civil war at the end of the last decade. Not to mention the NATO bombs falling from the sky. Jak's father had died many years before, and his grandmother said she was too old to go anywhere, but Jak, his brother Kostandin, and their mother were smuggled into the UK in the back of an animal-feed lorry. They settled in England for a few months but their application for asylum was rejected and they were interned at Beacon House Hospital awaiting deportation when the Christmas riot broke out. The boys were, at the time, both twelve years old. (There are eleven months between them.) Jak was asleep when the trouble began, and he got separated from his family. He never saw them again. He couldn't speak much English and was deported a few months later.

"Jak," I say, "this is awful."

"Yes," says Jak. "I was twelve years old and I'd lost my family. I was taken back to my country, where my people were at war with their own neighbours."

I can't imagine it at all.

"But it was OK; Granny kept me safe," says Jak.

"And I swore if I survived the war I'd come back to England one day to find out what happened to my mother and my brother."

I don't know if now is the right time to tell him what I think I know about his mother. Maybe Kos will tell him, when he's better.

At the hospital we are surrounded by paramedics and as Kos won't let go of my hand, I have to go with him. Jak comes too; he tells all the doctors he's his brother and everyone believes him. Poor Kos looks absolutely terrified. I swear if he was stronger he'd jump right out of the window.

"Jesus, who is this?" asks the doctor. He's about thirty and has got a bit of a goatee beard, which isn't great, but he's got twinkly blue eyes and nice clean hands. He tells us to call him Dr Paul.

"This is Kos," I say. "If you want him to like you, give him some food."

Kos has to be bribed with a sausage sandwich from the canteen before he lets Dr Paul look at his leg. A second sandwich allows him to clean it and after a third, he submits to bandaging and a painkilling injection. But when the medics start talking about X-rays and interpreters and assessments, Kos grabs my hand even harder.

"Polis?" he whispers.

"No polis," I say. "Kos safe."

Jak starts gabbling away, trying to talk to him, and

Kos closes his eyes with a pained look. It's as if he's trying to shut him out. "I'm his brother," says Jak in exasperation. "Why won't he talk to me?"

"Don't push it," I say quietly. "Give him time." I give Dr Paul Emily's number and tell him to get her to come here as soon as possible. Kos needs to see faces he trusts.

I think the painkillers Dr Paul gave him must be pretty strong because fairly soon, Kos, dressed in hospital pyjamas (still dirty, though; he wouldn't let them give him a bath) is fast asleep in a private room. Jak and Emily are waiting by his side with sandwiches and crisps for when he wakes up.

Mother and I are having a breather in the gardens outside the hospital. We've been told the police are on their way to interview us. There's a lot to say. I don't know how to begin.

"You realize this is all going to blow up," says Mother.

I nod, noticing how the rhinestones on her T-shirt sparkle in the white hospital lights. She gets her phone out of her bag. She fiddles with it for a while, then passes it to me. I hear a series of beeps, then a frightened voice.

"*Mum.*"

There's the sound of a door crashing open.

"*Get OUT!*"

"*Can I have a cuddle, Lexi?*"

"*No, you're pissed, Owen. Get out.*"

"But it's my last night of freedom. Come on, Lexi, I know you like me."

"I hate you. Fuck off and die."

"Just a little kiss."

The phone beeps and goes quiet. It recorded everything. "He's quite a handful," I say eventually. "Your fiancé." I give her back the phone and she grabs my hand.

"Are you all right?"

I tell her about Johnny coming in. I tell her I'm fine.

"Thank God," says Mother. "I'm so sorry, Lexi, I should never have left you." She'd been out dancing and hadn't got my messages until a couple of hours ago. Then, when I didn't answer her call, she made one of her friends drive her all the way home from Cornwall. She found the house empty and trashed. Then she'd got my text. She said she called Owen and me but there was no response. She managed to get hold of Johnny. He'd been wandering in the woods looking for me, but had got lost and ended up walking along the main road. He'd told her that Owen and his brothers were drunk and were hunting the tramp with guns. He told her that I was still up here somewhere. Mother drove out to meet Johnny and then came on to the old hospital.

They'd followed the sound of shouting and found us in the chapel.

Mother looks long and hard at me. "You need a bath," she says.

*

256

It's three weeks later.

Jak says there is still great tension in Kosovo, and NATO soldiers still patrol the streets, but the war is over and Kos is going to go home. He has a grandmother and a brother who are getting ready to cope with a man-boy who has lived in a derelict building, with pretty much only a pack of dogs for company, for three years. His grandmother, Sadja, has come over. I met her. She's tiny, wears a black headscarf and hardly speaks a word of English. She kept wringing my hand when she met me. Kos didn't exactly leap into her arms but he didn't run away either.

"*Kostandin*," was all she said.

Kos saw her and said, "*Gjyshee, mamaja.*"

When Jak heard this, he started crying. I had to look away then. I don't think I should have been there. They're all staying with Emily whilst they get used to each other and so that Jak can be a witness in court. Then they are all going home.

When I arrive for my second visit, Jak answers the door. Emily is in the kitchen, and Kos is asleep upstairs. Jak asks me to go out into the garden with him. I follow, intrigued. His grandmother is already out there, sitting on a bench and sipping a glass of water. She gets up and hugs me when she sees me. She smells of aniseed and old woman.

"What's the matter?" I ask Jak. "Do you want me to get your old job back or something?"

Jak looks me in the eyes. He really is like Kos in a

number of ways. They have the same hairline, the same lips. . .

"Lexi, I think there's things we don't know. Maybe you can help us?"

I get a little shock of alarm. I thought that everything was sorted. Kos is found and Owen has been arrested.

"Kos keeps talking about our mother," says Jak. I nod. That's fair enough. Their mother is at the centre of all of this. I found out that she was called Sazanna, but I still think of her as Mad-Bird.

"He says she was in the woods with him," says Jak. I nod again.

"Lexi, he says she *lived* in the woods with him."

"Maybe you didn't understand what he was saying," I say. Kos doesn't speak much, in English or in Albanian, his native language.

"No, he heard right." Emily stands in the doorway, leaning on her stick. She shuffles out to join us.

"Emily?"

The old woman blows her nose. "I knew it would come out," she says, sighing.

"What?" asks Jak. "What would come out?"

Emily sits on the bench next to Sadja.

"I found Kos in the forest, four days after the riot, and he led me to his mother. Sazanna had escaped during the riot. But some of the guards had followed her." Emily glances at me. "She'd been badly beaten. I think she'd been left for dead."

I press myself into the garden wall. Images of the

Neasdons and Owen, drunk, violent, and loose in the forest, race through my head.

"When I found her, she was sleeping in an abandoned car, up a rough track, deep in the forest. She was covered in bruises," Emily says. "But Sazanna wouldn't let me get help for her. She didn't trust the authorities, not after what she'd been through. And I didn't know what was the right thing to do. I felt so alone. Kos was just a boy, and Sazanna was. . ." Emily pauses. "Troubled."

Jak stares at Emily, his horror showing clearly on his face. Sadja gently tugs at his sleeve and he collects himself enough to translate to her what was being said.

"She was also in a bad way, up here." Emily taps her temple. "She was terrified of everything. So she and Kos hid out in the forest. And when the hospital closed down, they lived in the grounds. I bought them food and blankets and clothes, but Sazanna never really regained her strength." Emily wipes tears from her cheeks.

"She loved a particular clearing in the trees. She would lie on her back and look at the clouds. She said they'd flown over from home to say hello." Emily's voice cracks. "About a year after the riot, Kos found her lying there. At first he didn't think anything of it. But when he got closer, he saw that she was dead."

Nobody says anything. Next door a radio is blaring out pop tunes.

"That's very sad," I whisper.

Emily nods. "Kos was inconsolable. We buried her in the old swimming pool. I thought it was the best thing to do for Kos's sake. But the authorities found her soon after. It nearly broke Kos's heart when they took her away. It wasn't the wrong thing to do, was it?" She looks at everyone anxiously. "I've been so frightened that I did the wrong thing. That's why I haven't said anything. I worried that I should have done things differently."

After Jak translates Emily's speech to his grandmother, there is another long silence. I try to work it all out in my brain. Owen didn't murder Sazanna after all; he only *thought* he did. And he thought Kos saw him do it. That's why he wanted to get hold of him.

"If you'd got medical help, my mother would have lived," begins Jak in a harsh voice. But his grandmother puts her hand over his mouth. Then she touches Emily's shoulder and hugs her.

"Thank you," she says slowly in a strong accent, ". . .for looking after my children."

Famous

I don't want to be famous. I was never one of those crazy girls who used to sing R&B loudly in the hope they might get discovered and get catapulted from the school corridors to Wembley Stadium. But after this stuff with Kos, I've had my share of the limelight. I've had my photo taken by loads of newspapers and I've been offered loads of cash, I mean LOADS of cash, for "my story". I'm considering it. For a few days I had my picture on the front page of loads of papers. There were pictures of Kos too, looking grumpy and confused. Everyone is gawping at him so much I feel dead protective. It's good that he's got Emily and Jak and Sadja. Jak invited me to their country. He said to come in a couple of months or so. He said it would be good for Kos to have some continuity. Emily has said that if it doesn't work out he can always come and live with her. However, he'll have to get past British immigration before that can happen.

When I went to see them again last week, Kos was dressed in grey trousers and a woolly jumper. He was clean and had a short haircut. He wasn't my Kos any more. To think, all that time I wanted him to have a bath, I actually preferred him as he used to be. His face is changing too. It's filling out already. He looks younger. Jak says he's just nineteen; that's only three years older than me. He still looks like a lush bucket, but he's not my Kos any more. Now he's living in a normal-ish household, he's just plain crazy. He doesn't sleep much at night, but stalks around the house and garden, and Emily has to keep the fridge door locked or he eats all the food. He will not shave. He's addicted to cartoons. He has already stolen two dogs from Emily's neighbours and been made to return them. It's not going to be easy for any of them.

So I'm going to lose Kos. I don't know if I'm sad or not. Was he ever my boyfriend? *Come on, Lexi*, I tell myself. *You couldn't even talk to the man.* As I leave Emily's cottage I wave at Kos through the window and he blows me a kiss. Then he starts jumping up and down on the sofa.

Something nice happened last week. Mr Wellspring's collie, Zulu, came back from the grave. It was the talk of the village. Mr Wellspring said he'd got home and there the dog was, lying in the spot where his basket used to be. Mr Wellspring said he'd yelled so loudly that next door had come running over with his Neighbourhood Watch pager.

Zulu had been missing for just over a year.

Two days after that, another dog, Tess, the spaniel, came home after a three-month absence. And the next day Buttons the terrier returned. I suppose the pack was falling apart without Kos, their leader, to unite them. All this set all the other dog owners talking. After a consultation with me (I confirmed there had been at least seven dogs at large in the forest and mentioned the quarry) and in conjunction with two police vets, a supply of offal from the butchers and Mr Pepper's Flossy (she was in heat) there was a mass expedition to find them.

I didn't go. I'm still scared of the mantraps.

Working in the hotel, you get to hear everything, and I found out that by the end of the day, four dogs had been collected. Apparently they'd had to use tranquillizer darts on two of them: Maybelle, the big Alsatian, and Ziggy, the lurcher cross greyhound that I called Monster. These dogs were totally insane and were taken to RSPCA kennels in an attempt to re-domesticate them. I don't rate their chances. They know nothing except loving and protecting Kos.

We're moving out of Bewlea on Friday. Most of the boxes have been packed and crockery wrapped in newspaper. We've just got to take down the curtains and clean the house from top to bottom. Now that Owen has been arrested on suspicion of attempted murder, Mother and me thought we'd like to make a fresh start. Mother's found a two-bedroomed flat in a village between here and Bexton, which means she can keep working at the hotel, and I can finally start college. Most importantly, the two bedrooms mean there is no way Devlin can come and stay. Mother's going to rent out the house until she can sell it. She says when it sells me and her are going to New York because she thinks after recent events we both deserve a holiday.

"Thank goodness I hadn't paid out for the honeymoon," she said. She's not been especially sad about Owen. She said it was "never meant to be". And that she'd had doubts about the wedding even before all this.

"I'd hoped the wedding would fix things between us," she'd said. "But of course that's crazy. I see it now."

Mother has also set me up with some driving lessons because I turn seventeen next week. I hope the instructor isn't too surprised when they find out I can already drive.

Today is important because Kos and his family are due to fly home. Mother and I go to Emily's cottage to wave them off. There are lots of hugs and I confess I shed a tear or two. Even though I am NOT in love with Kos. Now that he's being fed regularly he's got quite fat in a very short space of time, and he bounds around like a little kid. Mother says he probably still has the mental age of a twelve-year-old. It's called arrested development. However, Kos and I have one last cuddle before he takes a crushed rose from his pocket and gives it to me with a smile.

I hope he's going to be all right.

264

"Just think," I say to Mother as Kos, his gran, Jak and Kos's social worker all climb into the taxi which will take them to the airport. "Dad and Owen might be cellmates. You've got such a bad track record with men."

"So have you," says Mother, watching as Kos presses his tongue to the window. It's a fair point. Kos is too mad, even for me. Emily, Mother and I stand on the verge and wave as the taxi departs. Kos waves through the back window. I blow him a kiss.

"Goodbye, Kos," I say.

I think he's going to be all right. He's got people around him who love him. That's not all he needs, but it's a good start. I have tears in my eyes. Mother looks over and squeezes my arm.

"You'll miss him, won't you?" she says.

But I'm not crying for him. I'm thinking about a woman who died in the forest, two years ago.

I'm thinking about Sazanna.

ALLY KENNEN comes from a proud lineage of bare-knuckle boxers, country vicars and French aristocracy. Prior to becoming a writer, she worked as an archaeologist, a giant teddy bear and a professional singer and songwriter.

Her first novel, BEAST, published in 2006, was shortlisted for the Booktrust Teenage Prize and the Carnegie Medal, and won the 2007 Manchester Book Award. Her second novel, BERSERK, won the North-East Teenage Book Award and the Leicester Book of the Year Award 2008. Her third novel, BEDLAM, has been longlisted for the Carnegie Medal.

Ally lives in Somerset with her husband, three small children, four chickens, and a curmudgeonly cat.

No woman has ever beaten Ally in an arm wrestle.

Also by Ally Kennen

BEAST
BEDLAM

SPARKS